Fire and Ice

"We never told you about Nell," Lara said to Celeste as they approached the house. "She was one of the gang when we were all small. She moved away when we were in fourth grade."

"Nell hasn't had the easiest life," Dana added quietly.

"Why?" Celeste asked.

"When we were nine years old," Lara began, "Nell had an accident."

"It was nobody's fault," Dana interjected.

"She got burned," Lara continued. "Her face and hands. She had to have extensive plastic surgery, which was very painful. She looks okay now, but it's always there between us. You see, the accident that burned her — each one of us contributed to it." Lara tried to smile to relieve her tension. "I guess you would call it our deep, dark secret."

"Was anyone else hurt?" Celeste asked, stooping down to make a snowball. Obviously she did not notice how badly the topic disturbed them.

"No," Dana said quickly.

Do not talk about it. Do not remember.

"No one else," Lara echoed weakly; not exactly a lie. Nicole hadn't really been hurt. Nicole had died.

point

Slumber Party

Christopher Pike

SCHOLASTIC INC.
New York Toronto London Auckland Sydney

Library of Congress Cataloging in Publication Data

Pike, Christopher.
  Slumber party.

  (A Point paperback)
  Summary: When a ski weekend reunites a group
of teenage girls eight years after a fire at a slumber
party disfigured one of them and killed her sister,
new fire-related accidents suggest that one of them
may have been responsible.
  [1. Horror stories. 2. Mystery and detective stories]
I. Title.
PZ7.P626Sl 1985   [Fic]   84-20238

ISBN 0-590-43014-9

11 10 9 8 7   1 2 3 4/9

Printed in the U.S.A.   01

Slumber Party

Chapter 1

Dana Miller's downshifting, as they rounded the tight mountain turn, was like a kick in the seat of the pants. The plowed snow looming above their VW gave the illusion of being in a bobsled run. The dazzling white landscape was more than unshielded eyes could bear, but here in the shade, Lara Johnson stared out the window in delightful awe. This weekend ski trip would be one of the high points of her life.

"How am I doing?" Dana asked, referring to her driving.

"Well. . . ." Lara began, not wishing to offend her oldest and best friend. "We are still alive."

Dana chuckled. "Does that mean you want me to slow down?"

The back wheels zigzagged as they whipped out of another turn. "A bit," Lara breathed, putting a hand on the dashboard.

"I wouldn't mind being late," Celeste Winston agreed from the backseat, reopening her eyes slowly.

Dana sighed, putting on the brake, "Doesn't look like we have much choice. The road's blocked off."

A hundred yards in front, a chain was suspended across the asphalt, behind which rose a miniature mountain of snow. Three cars were jammed into a makeshift parking lot. A ranger waved them to the side. Dana buried the front end of the car before she could kill their momentum on the ice-slick surface. Lara rolled down her window.

"We're heading to Cedar Stream," she said. "Is there another way around?"

The man tugged on his white whiskers, a Colonel Sanders clone. "You must be with them other young ladies," he said, in a country-boy voice.

Dana nudged her side, pointing at a parked BMW. "There's Rachael's car," she said.

Lara nodded. "We are. Do you know how long ago they got here?"

"Must be — ohh — near two hours ago."

"That Rachael drives like a fiend," Dana said.

"She's not alone," Lara muttered.

"This is as close as you're going to get," the ranger said, answering her initial question. "But Cedar Stream's only three miles away. You got cross-country skis, I see. Should have no trouble hiking in."

Lara felt a pang of concern for Celeste.

At school she wasn't allowed to take PE because of a bad back. Indeed, since this was primarily a skiing trip, Celeste should not have come. But upon hearing of their plans, their younger friend had pleaded to be included, if only to enjoy the scenery.

"I'll be okay," Celeste said, meeting her eyes.

"You have no skis," Lara said.

"I'll walk. I walk pretty good."

"If the snow's powdery," Dana said, "you'll swim."

Lara put on sunglasses and climbed out of the car. Drifts had cut many of the pines to pint size. The miles they would have to master did not appear an easy proposition.

"There is a packed path yonder this ridge," the ranger uttered, reading her mind. He frowned as Dana dug open the hood and began to unload their supplies. He said, "Like I told your friends, you best be well stocked with food. By night, a granddaddy of a storm is going to hit."

"I told you," Dana said, tossing Celeste a duffel bag, who caught it and promptly disappeared giggling into a wall of snow.

"Careful, careful," Lara said. "I know, Dana. I read the papers, too. I told Nell we should wait until next weekend, but she insisted that it had to be this weekend. So did Rachael, for that matter."

"Rachael's just hoping that you break a leg so you'll end up in the hospital and be out of running for homecoming queen," Dana said, not joking. "I still think she was the one responsible for me getting kicked off the Associated Student Body Council."

"If they put a cast over my face, maybe she would stand a chance," Lara said, not taking herself seriously. Rachael would win hands down: tall, blond, tan — she looked like a cover girl. What could a short, dark-haired nobody with fifties bangs and a nose that was at least — despite what her friends said — a size too large do against a Barbie Doll? Of course, personality wise, Rachael was not everyone's dream queen. "What do we do with our car?" Lara asked the man, who was following their exchange with a wry grin.

"Leave the keys. A partner of mine and I will move them down to the lodge."

"That's awfully nice of you," Lara said, surprised. Didn't rangers have more important things to do? "What name should we mention when we pick it up?" She couldn't find a badge.

"The colonel," the man smiled, smoothing his whiskers again.

The effort required to balance a duffle bag on her back, while simultaneously trying to recall seldom-used cross-country ski techniques, caused muscles to ache that Lara hadn't even known she had. Yet as she paused to catch her breath and wipe off the beads of perspiration dripping into her eyes, she realized that she hadn't felt this exhilarated in ages. The air was so crisp and sweet that it was like biting into a dessert. In every direction, the scenery could have been framed and pasted on a postcard. The flawless blue sky made it difficult to take seriously the warning of an approaching storm.

"If I died and couldn't get into heaven," Dana said, "I wouldn't mind spending the rest of eternity here." Her back was bent with a weight similar to what Lara was carrying. Only Celeste, who moved gingerly between them on a ski track, stood erect. She had valiantly tried to help, but they had ended up digging her out of the snow.

"Quite a change from West Star High," Lara agreed, which was where the three of them went to school, in the heart of congested Oakland.

"Maybe we'll meet some guys," Dana said hopefully. With a great deal of fondness, Lara had to admit that Dana's face was one best loved by a mother. Yet Dana had no shortage of boyfriends, only a lack of ones that — as Dana put it — appreciated her from the neck up.

"Six single girls," Lara said. "We'll have to meet a whole herd of them." Though she would settle for one. She hadn't gone out on a date in six weeks. At first she had thought that she was being too picky, but then again, she hadn't said no to anybody.

"What we need is a party," Dana said. "The storm can strand whoever comes."

Lara noticed ever-silent Celeste blushing, and asked, "Do you date much?"

Celeste was startled by the question. "Oh, I've never gone out with a boy."

"You should," Dana said. "They need us. Believe me."

"I . . . can't," Celeste replied hesitantly.

"Won't your aunt let you?" Lara asked.

"She. . . . I don't think she would mind."

"You're too shy, is that it?" Lara asked gently.

Celeste looked at the ground. It seemed as if an envelope of sorrow had enfolded her. "Yeah, that's why," she said finally.

Lara thought that there was more to the matter. The doubt forced her to evaluate just how scant their knowledge of Celeste was.

On what had been only the second day of school, Lara had been browsing in the library for something to read. Working at the local mall's theaters during the week was an exercise in killing time. She had picked up a Stephen King horror novel and was reading the critics' raves on the inside flap, when she noticed a slight, pale, auburn-haired girl, staring at either her or the book. What struck Lara from the first instant was the innocence of her expression.

Lara smiled at her and waved the book. "Have you read this?"

The girl approached slowly. Although the weather was warm, she was bundled up. Later Lara learned that Celeste always dressed this way.

"I've read all his books," she said in a small girl's voice.

"Do you get nightmares?"

The girl did not appear to connect the question with the reference to the horror books. "I used to have many dreams about —" She frowned. "Oh, I see. No, books never scare me."

"What's your name?"

"Celeste."

"I'm Lara. You're new here."

"I am, yes."

"What grade are you in?"

"I'm a sophomore."

"A shame. I'm a senior. We can't be seen together." Celeste looked as though she had been slapped. Lara squeezed her arm. "I was only joking, for goodness' sake! Hey, I was just going to lunch. Have you eaten?"

"No."

"Are you hungry?"

"Yes."

"Good. I'm taking you to lunch."

Afterward Lara was not sure why she had felt such immediate warmth for Celeste. Perhaps it was the girl's obvious frailness that had awakened a desire to protect.

Over lunch Lara had asked why she had been staring at her. Celeste had replied, "You looked nice."

Her tone had been filled with amazement.

Since then Celeste had revealed few personal facts. Her parents were dead. She lived alone with her aunt. She had a bad back from a car accident. She liked books.

"There it is!" Dana exclaimed, as they crested a frozen bluff. The trilevel frame house was set in the side of a natural granite wall, spacious windows opening on a breathtaking view of the valley. A thin trail of smoke drifted from a towering brick chimney. Home sweet home. They plopped down their burdens.

"Can you imagine the bucks Nell's parents must have to buy a place like that?" Dana asked with a mixture of disdain and envy.

"Money isn't everything," Celeste said.

Dana stared at her. "Were you just hatched from an egg?"

"We never told you about Nell," Lara said to Celeste. "She was one of the gang when we were all small. She moved away when we were in fourth grade. Her family's in oil. They live in Sacramento now. Over the years, she's kept in contact. She's a good friend."

"When you meet her," Dana said, "don't mind her seriousness. That's just the way she is." She added quietly, "Nell hasn't had the easiest life."

"Why?" Celeste asked.

Lara and Dana exchanged looks. Fourth grade — long enough ago for everyone's memory to fade, except for Nell's. The facial scars she saw in every mirror made that impossible. She hadn't moved away. She had been driven away.

Except for the addition of Celeste, and the absence of Nell's younger sister, Nicole, this weekend's cast would be the same as *that* slumber party.

"When we were nine years old," Lara began, "Nell had an accident."

"It was nobody's fault," Dana interjected.

"She got burned," Lara continued. "Her face and hands. She had to have extensive plastic surgery, which was very painful. She looks okay now, but it's always there between us. You see, the accident that burned her — each of us contributed to it." Lara tried to smile to relieve her tension. "I guess you would call it our deep, dark secret."

"Was anyone else hurt?" Celeste asked, stooping down to make a snowball. Obviously she did not notice how badly the topic disturbed them.

"No," Dana said quickly, before Lara could speak. "No one else was hurt."

Dana pressed Lara with her eyes, shaking her head. The thought was mutual.

Do not talk about it. Do not remember.

"No one else," Lara echoed weakly; not exactly a lie. Nicole hadn't really been hurt. Nicole had died.

"I'll be especially nice to her," Celeste promised.

"Hey you penguins!!" came a shout from the house, "What took you so long?"

Mindy Casey, tripping over her scarf and enthusiasm, floundered toward them. In appearance she was a pale shadow of her idol — Rachael. Her character took after her bubble-gum chewing obsession: initially sweet, often swelled with hot air, periodically exploding. Lara couldn't imagine life without her.

"Give me that snowball," Dana said, taking Celeste's embryonic snowman and unleashing a pitch that grazed Mindy's forehead.

"I just did my makeup!" Mindy cried, wiping her face. A brief but furious snowball fight ensued. Outnumbered two to one — Celeste did not participate — Mindy soon surrendered. As part of their terms, she helped them with their bags to the house.

"Was there much work getting this place livable?" Lara asked.

"Nell's been slaving away, though she did have us clean out the basement, but Rachael and I spent most of our time on a snowman," Mindy said. "He's on the other side of the house, wearing that scarf your mother knitted Rachael when she was a kid, and my cowboy hat and sunglasses. He looks new wave."

Rachael Grayson appeared on the porch.

"Hi, girls," she said in her slightly cynical tone that made the uninitiated feel that they weren't quite as important as they thought they were. Seeing Rachael, poster perfect in her skin-tight, blue ski outfit and dazzling shower of blond hair, Lara thought again how ludicrous it was that they were in competition.

"Look at you," Dana said in disgust. "No way I'm going to go hustle guys with you."

Rachael smiled faintly, acknowledging her physical superiority. "How are you, *Princess Lara?*" she asked.

"Just perfect, *Princess Rachael*," Lara mimicked. Both of them had already been elected to the homecoming court. "Where is our loyal subject, Nell?"

"Preparing our royal chambers, poor wench," Rachael said, causing them all to laugh. Rachael came down the steps and hugged them.

"You must drive like a fiend," Dana said.

"We left before dawn. Had to pick up Nell. You should see her house. It should have a moat."

"How is she?" Lara asked quietly.

Rachael wobbled her palm. "So, so. She has

a slight fever. I think it's caused by having us all here at once. I think it . . . you know what I mean."

"What did you think of the storm Colonel Sanders is worried about?" Dana asked.

Rachael laughed. "What's a few more snowflakes in this icebox?"

"Those few more snowflakes could bury us here for days," Dana said. "We told you to wait till next weekend."

A cold light hardened Rachael's eyes. Since childhood Lara had sensed, but never witnessed, a part of Rachael capable of genuine violence. "It was important that we come this weekend," Rachael said flatly.

"Hello," Nell Kutroff said, causing everyone to jump slightly. She was standing in the doorway, bracing herself against the railing. Wrinkles of fatigue pinched her eyes. The scars about her nose and mouth were more noticeable than usual. This was the first time since the accident that Lara had seen Nell without heavy makeup.

"How are you?" Dana asked tentatively, not moving from her spot.

"Fine. It's good to see you again, Dana. Real good."

Lara felt herself drawn involuntarily forward. She hugged Nell tightly. Nell hesitated before returning the gesture. Unshed tears burned Lara's eyes. Why this sudden depth of emotion? Was it a flood of relief or guilt? They separated, studying each other. "You look good," Lara said finally, lying. It was guilt.

Nell smiled. "You look better."

Lara put her hand on Nell's forehead. "But you've got a fever." Actually she didn't feel hot at all.

She shrugged. "I'll be all right after a nap. I prepared your rooms. You each have your own, and they're all on the top floor."

"Thanks," Lara said.

"I wanted to congratulate you on being one of the top five beauties at school," Nell said formally.

"I campaigned vigorously," Lara said. The compliment was but another reminder. Nell would have, should have, been beautiful.

Celeste was hiding behind Rachael and Mindy. Lara beckoned for her. "This is the wonderful new friend that I told you all about on the phone. Nell, meet Celeste."

For the longest moment neither made a move nor spoke. Finally Nell offered her hand. "That's a beautiful name, Celeste," she said, with a trace of nervousness. "What does it mean?"

"Nothing," Celeste said.

"Heavenly," Lara corrected. Surely Celeste must have known that!

"I'm glad you could come," Nell said.

"I appreciate you having me," Celeste said.

There was a strained undercurrent on both sides. Lara wondered if Celeste's coming was an imposition on Nell. She said: "Celeste has back trouble so she won't be skiing with us. She can guard the fort."

"Speaking of which," Rachael said. "No offense meant, but I didn't come here just to shoot the bull with you ladies. Let's hit the slopes!"

"How far are the lifts?" Mindy asked.

"About four miles," Nell said. "But there's an excellent hard-packed path the entire way. Leads right to the door of the lodge. I'll show you on a map."

"Aren't you coming with us?" Lara asked.

Nell wiped her forehead. "I think I'll rest a bit first. I can join you later. Now come, let me show you your rooms."

They were taken on a tour of how the other half lived. Each bedroom was ridiculously large. The central fireplace — there were three altogether — could have roasted a prize steer. The constant smell of pine and cedar was a pleasure. They didn't go into the basement, but Nell told them of a recently installed propane tank that could supply them with enough power to endure the fiercest winter siege.

Lara was concerned that Nell did not feel well enough to accompany them, but she was pleased that Celeste would not have to be left alone. Hopefully they would hit it off.

Before leaving, Rachael and Mindy insisted that the rest of them see their snowman. They exited through a side door, where the snow was shaded by the house.

But there was no snowman.

The scarf, sunglasses, and cowboy hat rested on the ground.

"Mindy," Rachael said, annoyed.

"I didn't knock it down!"

"Well, I'm sure Nell didn't," Rachael said.

"I haven't been out of the house since we arrived," Nell said, puzzled.

"Is this some kind of adolescent prank?" Dana accused Mindy.

"No! I swear. Somebody else must have knocked it down."

"A psychotic snowman murderer with an ax, right," Rachael said.

"The only tracks are ones that lead from the house," Nell said.

"It must have melted," Mindy said.

"Impossible," Nell said. "It was in the shade. And besides, it's too cold."

Lara stooped to gather up the late snowman's clothes. The scarf and hat came loose only with a sharp yank. They had been frozen in place. A concave circle of ice about six feet in diameter had taken the place of the snowman.

"He *must* have melted," Lara said, "and taken some of the surrounding snow with him. And then froze again. See how smooth it is here?"

Rachael frowned. "Weird."

Lara asked Nell, "Is there a pipe or a vent under this spot?"

"Definitely not."

"There must be," Rachael insisted. "The pipe could be underground."

Nell shook her head. "I've been coming here since I was a child. I would know."

"How the hell did he melt, then?" Rachael demanded.

"Probably saw a nude female snowman and got too hot," Dana suggested.

That broke them up. They began back toward the house. Except for Lara. She remained studying the impression of ice. It was as though the snowman had suddenly caught fire.

"I'm hungry," Dana growled.

"You're always hungry," Lara said.

"I wish anorexia was contagious and I knew someone who could infect me."

"Wonder what's taking them so long?"

They were sitting in the lounge next to a heating vent, their recently rented downhill skis standing sentinels on either side. Rachael and Mindy were still being fitted. Nell had provided them with lift passes. The trip down from the house had been uneventful. However, dark clouds could now be seen to the northeast.

"Rachael's probably having her skis shined to where she can see her face whenever she looks down," Dana said.

"I heard that," Rachael snapped, striding into the room, Mindy on her tail, both empty-handed.

"Where are they?" Lara asked.

"We're picking up the skis in a bit," Rachael said. "Mindy and I have some things we want to do first."

"What are these *things*?" Lara asked.

"We're meeting some friends," Mindy said, popping a bubblegum balloon.

"You can meet friends in Oakland," Dana said, sounding vaguely jealous. "Let's ski first."

"But you're hungry, Dana," Rachael said with profound concern. "You need your nourishment or you'll starve that cute double chin of yours." Dana stuck out her tongue. Rachael added, "Seriously, Lara, why don't you two eat? We shouldn't be too long."

Rachael and Mindy began to walk away as if the matter were settled, which annoyed Lara. "Is this why this weekend was so important?" she called.

They just giggled, and were gone.

"Do I really have a double chin?" Dana asked.

"Of course not."

"You liar. Let's go stuff our faces."

The coffee shop was jammed. Ski parkas from every color of the rainbow, and ski chatter from overactive imaginations filled the room. They had to wait to be seated. Dana decided on the entire menu before finally ordering a chicken cashew sandwich and a large piece — as she made clear to the waitress with her hands — of chocolate cake.

Lara had a bowl of vegetable soup. She was dieting. She was always dieting. Damn that Rachael, she didn't deserve to be homecoming queen.

"I read in a magazine that skiing burns seven hundred and fifty calories a minute," Dana said in between mouthsful of food. "You sure you don't want some cake?"

"An hour."

"Huh?"

"Seven hundred and fifty calories an hour. I read the same magazine."

"Does that mean you don't want a piece of cake?"

Lara put a hand on her stomach. "I am still hungry. Maybe an apple will kill the urge."

At the fruit bowl, all the apples were green, so she decided on an orange instead. She had picked up and squeezed half a dozen when a soft male voice spoke behind her.

"Are you looking for a hard one, or a soft one?"

The question made her jump and drop her orange. He picked it up and placed it aside on the table. "I guess you don't want this one," he smiled.

Lara managed to shake her head. He was a few years older, and half a foot taller, than herself. His olive skin wasn't from overexposure to the mountain sun. He was of either Greek or Slavic descent, yet he had light green eyes, which contrasted sharply with a shock of unmanaged black hair. He was vaguely frightening, definitely handsome.

"The reason I ask," he continued, "is because I often see people squeezing oranges and I never know what they're looking for."

If this was a come-on, it was rather clever. "I was looking for one that was neither too hard nor too soft," Lara said.

"Up for the day?"

"The weekend."

"Supposed to snow heavily tonight."

"I know."

"Where are you staying?"

Lara nodded and smiled. "That-a way, at a friend's house. I'm with some girls from school."

Her hint that she wasn't with a guy removed a subtle barrier. He smiled again. He had nice teeth. "I'm Percy Chand."

She shook his hand. "Lara Johnson, pleased to meet you. Where are you from . . . Percy?"

"Currently, San Francisco. But I'm never in one place long."

"I'm from Oakland."

"I was there a couple of weeks ago. Do you go to school there, or what?"

The question was really, are you still in high school? "For another few months," Lara said vaguely.

Percy reached randomly into the fruit bowl. "This couple looks good. Can I join you?"

"Well . . . I am with a friend. I would have to ask her."

"My buddy should be along in a minute. We're already bored with each other."

"I . . . I guess it would be okay."

She led Percy to the table. Dana's eyes sparkled when she saw him. She stretched her neck to flatten any undue bulges. "Dana, this is Percy. He's from San Francisco." She tossed in, "He's here with a friend."

"Hi!" Dana said, a shade too loud.

"Hello."

With introductions complete, they sat down. The conversation flowed easily. Lara and Dana did most of the talking. Percy possessed the rare virtue of being a good listener. His interest in both of them seemed genuine. When asked a question, even a frivolous one, he thought for a moment before answering, taking them seriously. His personality was soft. He was originally from Canada, an orphan who hadn't gotten past ninth grade. Since leaving his foster home, he had spent most of his days drifting through the Western states, working enough to get by, then moving on. Currently he drove a truck for a furniture warehouse in San Francisco. Nevertheless, he assured them that he had a great ambition. He just hadn't figured out what it was yet. He was twenty-two.

Lara liked him. She could feel the symptoms of that magic haze, where the world was suddenly much brighter and more interesting. But afraid of the hurt of disappointment, she tried not to indulge her fantasies. After all, he was just a guy. . . .

"You sound like you've had an interesting life," Lara said. "Have you found it a handicap not having finished school?"

"Haven't picked a rotten orange yet," he smiled.

"Tell me about your friend," Dana said.

Percy hesitated. "Cal? He's more of a partner than a friend. I haven't known him long. I needed a place to stay and he had an available room. He's a character. Speak of the devil. There he is in the lobby. Be back in a sec."

With Percy gone, Lara asked, "What do you think?"

"That you're a lucky s.o.b. Hope his friend's got a fraction of his charm."

"How do you know it isn't you he likes?"

"I noticed no obvious symptoms of brain damage. Hey, remember what I said about a party? Let's invite these two up to the house. What with Rachael's and Mindy's fellows, we could have a blast."

"What about Nell and Celeste? This is supposed to be a slumber party, not an orgy."

"We won't let them stay. We have the whole night to slumber."

"I don't know," Lara said, drumming the table with her nails. She was more than tempted. Her hormones were being very persuasive. "If we suggest it, they might get the wrong idea. I'd have to ask Nell."

"Call her!"

"You haven't even met the guy!"

Dana laughed. "Has that ever stopped me?"

"I'll think about it."

Cal was a huge redhead with a massive mouth, the antithesis of Percy. He straddled a chair and waved his tongue nonstop for fifteen minutes about what fantastic skiers the two of them were. Dana appeared to like him well enough. She probably didn't notice him eyeing her breasts. Suddenly he stood.

"Got to go, got to unload the van." He asked Dana, "Want to come?"

"Sure."

"Catch you in a few minutes," Percy said as they left. When they were out of hearing range he looked at Lara and sighed. "Just an acquaintance, you understand."

"How old is Cal?"

Percy shrugged. "I'm not sure. He spent four years in the service so he's got to be at least twenty-two. Told me once — I think he was joking — that he got a discharge for *playing* with napalm."

"Is she safe with him?"

"He won't do any permanent damage," Percy muttered absently. He touched her arm. "I'm sorry, that was crude. She should be fine."

"Maybe I should be more worried for Cal."

"Can I see you again?" Percy asked abruptly.

"I would like that," Lara said slowly, racing inside.

"When?"

"We could go skiing together."

Percy shook his head. "Cal may have exaggerated, but we do ski off the top."

"But they call that Kamikaze Run. It starts like this." Lara held her hand at a ninety-degree angle. "What happens if you fall?"

"You roll to the bottom of the mountain. Don't looked so worried. I've skied here before."

Lara took a deep breath. "My girl friends will probably be having some guys over this evening. If you and Cal would like to come, I'm sure it would be okay. But I'll have to check with Nell — she's the one who owns the house — first."

"Great. We can bring drinks."

Worried that maybe she was getting in over her head, Lara excused herself to use the phone. Nell had written down the number for her before they had left.

"Hello, Nell? How are you feeling?"

"Fine."

"That's good. How are you and Celeste getting along?"

"We — we had a long talk."

"I'm glad. The reason I called, and don't hesitate to say no if you want to, is that the four of us met some guys and we were wondering if we could invite them up for the evening? Just for a little while?"

Nell did not answer immediately. Lara was on the verge of telling her to forget it, when Nell said, "I wouldn't mind. Let me ask, ahhh . . . let me ask. . . ."

"Celeste."

"Yeah, let me ask Celeste." Nell was gone an eternity. Finally: "Celeste says that it's fine with her but not to bother finding her a boy."

Lara chuckled. "How about you?"

"Bring whatever's available."

"Coming skiing with us?"

"Maybe."

Lara knew that she would never come. "Good-bye, Nell."

"Have fun, Lara."

Such melancholy in her voice, it tugged at Lara's heart. "We'll try to get back early," she promised.

Percy was happy with the news. She gave him detailed directions to the house and tactfully mentioned that they all wanted to get to bed early.

They had scarcely began to chat again when Rachael and Mindy slid onto the scene.

"Percy!" Rachael exclaimed. "So there you are! Where's Cal?"

Oh no, Lara thought. She braced herself for a scene.

Percy stood awkwardly. "Hi, Rachael,

Mindy. What are you — Cal's with Dana."

Mindy's bubble gum slipped out of her mouth and fell on the floor. "With *Dana*?"

Rachael took a seat. "Have you met my friend, Lara?"

"We've met," Lara muttered. Percy nodded, sinking back into his chair.

"Great," Rachael said brightly, casting her a microsecond glance that communicated a reservoir of hate. "I'm glad you could come, Percy."

"I didn't know you were coming," he said, smiling. "Definitely, I mean." He had regained his poise. He could see the humor in the situation.

"How did you two run into each other?" Rachael asked Lara.

"Well —" Lara began, not getting far.

"We met at the fruit bowl," Percy said matter-of-factly.

"You met at the fruit bowl." Rachael's pronunciation was very distinct.

"Is Cal coming back?" Mindy asked.

Percy laughed, standing. "I think that I had better go get him. Time we hit the snow." He nodded at her. "See you tonight. Good-bye, Rachael, Mindy."

"Take care," Lara whispered.

"Tonight?" Rachael asked. "What's tonight?"

"There's a party at your house," Percy smiled. "Everyone break a leg." He went to the cashier and paid for the oranges. He left without looking back. Considering the altitude, the air at the table was very thick.

"Nice guy," Lara said finally, shredding orange peels with her fingernails.

"Where's Dana?" Mindy whined.

"Oh, shut up, you!" Rachael said. "Dana's with Cal. Cal's with Dana. They're together in the same spot. Isn't that right, Lara?"

Lara bit her lip, and waved her hand impotently. "This is crazy. I just ran into him by accident."

"At the fruit bowl," Rachael spat.

"I didn't know he was with you," Lara said, raising her voice.

"And I suppose while the two of you were talking, my name was never mentioned!?"

"Right! Why should we talk about you?"

"Because it was me he was supposed to meet!"

"So he got lucky!"

"Why you little tramp!"

"Why you bigger one!"

"How long has Dana been with Cal?" Mindy asked.

Lara began to laugh hysterically. "Long enough, Mindy. Long enough."

There was a pause. Rachael asked with a slow razor: "Why did you invite him up to the house?"

Lara stopped laughing and stared Rachael right in the eye. "Because Nell said that it was okay."

"Because Nell said that it was okay?"

Lara scratched her head. "Are we getting an echo in here?"

"Shut up, Lara." Rachael smoldered, blood burning her face. "Goddamn that Percy."

"I'm sorry," Lara said gently, not altogether sincerely. "When did you meet them?"

"At the mall, a couple of weeks ago," Mindy said miserably.

"This is just like a soap opera," Lara said. "Always hated those shows."

Yet the best was still to come.

"What a creep!" Dana swore, dropping in on their merry group. Her hair and makeup were a mess. "I'm five minutes in that guy's room, helping him unpack, you understand, when he sneaks up behind me and begins to maul me like a — like an octopus. What does he think I am!? I should call a cop, or a ranger, or something. For your sake, Lara, I'm glad that Percy said that Cal wasn't really a friend. Rachael, Mindy, you would had to have seen this guy."

"They have," Lara told the ceiling. "They have."

"Did you sleep with Cal?!" Mindy screamed, bursting into tears. (Mindy suffered from the classically feminist-deficient upbringing. It was never the guy's fault.) They were suddenly the coffee shop's center of attraction.

Dana was mystified. "Huh?"

"Rach, she —" Mindy began.

"Don't say it," Rachael interrupted calmly.

She took Mindy's hand and stood. Her last words were devoid of emotion. "Looks like it will be an interesting slumber party, Lara."

"Never a dull moment," she agreed.

"See you on the mountain," Rachael said. Practically carrying Mindy, she left.

Dana watched them go in wonder. "I must have missed something."

"You'd be amazed," Lara said.

Chapter 2

This high point of Lara's life was pretty low. The skiing was no different than running laps in PE. She slid down the mountain, rode back up the mountain, slid down again. She was more conscious of her aching legs than of the fun she was supposed to be having. The wind had begun to blow and her hands were freezing. It was all Rachael's fault.

Staring at her dangling skis and the crisscrossed snow thirty yards below her lift chair, Lara figured that if Dana and she did not come to terms with Rachael and Mindy soon, the whole weekend would be shot. Neither side had spoken to the other since lunch, timing their lift rides to maintain a respectable, hostile distance. It was three o'clock. The sun would be setting early. Soon they would have to return to the house and prepare for the party.

Lara wondered if she should find Percy,

tell him to forget the whole thing. Dana had said she wasn't looking forward to a second wrestling session with Cal. Yet such a prospect left Lara feeling flatter than she did already. Daydreaming had spun in her head a book-length "soon-to-be" affair with Percy. He would call her when she returned home, ask her out, pick her up in a Porsche, take her to an expensive restaurant and order lobster, then to the theater, kissing her passionately in his leather upholstered seats afterward, promising that he would see her the following day, and the day after that. She was still working on the castle-in-the-sky and the happily-ever-after chapters. It was incredible the material an innocent, half-hour conversation could generate. A shame to kiss it all good-bye, without having even gotten to kiss Percy, merely to appease Rachael.

Of course, the party, with Rachael's full armament of charm on display, would probably be a more painful death to her dreams.

Lara hopped from the ski lift. Her thoughts elsewhere, she immediately fell hard on her rear-end, jarring her spine and not doing a damn thing for the pressure she already had inside her skull. Standing up took four frustrating tries. Finally, dusting snow off her jeans, she searched for and found Dana approaching, ten seats down on the lift. Dana trod down the run as if she had an orthopedic surgeon perched on her shoulder whispering paranoid warnings. Lara had gotten fed up waiting for her.

"That was a cute fall you took," Dana said, waddling to her side, sporting wide sunglasses designed to hide her big nose.

"Too bad you didn't have your camera," Lara said, none too pleasantly.

"Serves you right for not waiting for me. Hell, I've fallen on my butt a dozen times already. You don't see me crying."

"Yeah, but you've got built-in shock absorbers."

"Now Lara, that was low. Say you're sorry and I will forgive you. If the two of us start fighting, then we're really in trouble. Everyone else hates us."

Lara pulled off her wool cap and foggy sunglasses, brushing hair out of her eyes. Immediately the wind began to sting her ears. The once distant clouds on the horizon had gathered gray overhead, putting the landscape through a black and white filter. "Sorry," she said quietly.

"I forgive you. Come on, Lara, what is it? Or need I ask?"

"Do you think we should swallow our pride and put up the white flag?"

Dana shielded her eyes, peering in the direction of the lodge. "They're getting on the lift. If we wait here, they will come to us."

"We will wait."

"What are you going to say? You won't get to first base unless you call off the party."

Lara shook her head. "You've got it wrong. Even from a distance, I can feel Rachael's confidence. She's looking forward to the party. She thinks that when Percy sees the two of us together, he'll have no trouble with his selection." Lara fitted her cap back on, sighing, "And she's probably right."

Dana touched her arm. "You really like him? I mean, *really*?"

Lara's shoulders slumped. "I think I've talked myself into it."

"You need to see the *Rocky* films again. You're giving up without a fight. Surely Percy has enough sense to pick a sweetheart over a 'swelled-head.' "

"Assuming that I'm not the swelled-head, when have you ever seen a guy want my sweetness over her body?"

Dana paused. "Never. Still, there's no problem. Find Percy, tell him that Nell's changed her mind about the party, and give him your phone number. Don't give Rachael another shot at him."

"No good. First I'd have to find him, which would be next to impossible. Still, even if I could find him, and he did ask me for my number, Rachael would know what I'd done, that I was afraid to compete with her."

"This sounds like an athletic contest. If you want, I'll be the one to call it off. They know I despise Cal."

"Do you really? You don't say that with much conviction."

"You think I enjoyed being mauled?"

"Did you?"

"Lara!"

"Did you?"

"None of your business. Just let me call it off. Forget your having to compete on even terms with Rachael. She's got a ten-point edge going in."

"No."

"You're being dumb."

"I know. But I want to see him. I miss him already."

Dana was sympathetic. "You've fallen, sister. I hope he wants to catch you. It doesn't matter what we decide anyway. They'll be here in a sec. Let's just feel our way."

Rachael and Mindy knew that they were waiting for them, despite their phony self-absorbed conversation that was designed to deny their existence. Only when Rachael had stepped off the lift, stretched, brushed her hair, and yawned, did she grace them with a passing glance. Mindy was not so subtle, showing them her back. Lara knew she would have to take the initiative.

"Hello," she said, "oldest and best friends."

Rachael's expression was calculating. "Are you being sarcastic, Lara?"

"Not at all. Been having fun?"

Mindy turned slowly. Rachael appeared to

drop her guard a notch. She said, "This snow's divine. We've been having a great time."

"A super time." Mindy put in.

"We'd like to offer a truce," Lara said.

Rachael was back in command. "Really, Lara, don't be so dramatic. So we like the same guy. So what? This isn't a war. Me, I'm kind of looking forward to tonight. Like you said, never a dull moment. We'll have a great time."

"I think we should call it off," Dana muttered, looking at her.

Rachael understood and smiled. "No way," she said.

"Fine with me," Lara shrugged, her heart sinking. Rachael would flash her ultra-bright smile when he looked at her, run her sharp nails through her golden hair and accidentally brush his leg when she sat beside him, laugh deep and sexy in her throat and lean into his side with her firm breasts when he told a joke, let her crystal blue eyes slip from his spellbound stare to his crotch, letting him know that with her possibilities were endless. Percy would come a-running. Lara felt profoundly sad. Just this once, she had hoped. . . . At least she would get to see him again.

The four of them began to cut their way down the mountain. Dana and Mindy teamed up — both being mediocre skiers — and fell behind, seemingly on speaking terms again.

The last words Lara heard of their conversation were Dana reassuring Mindy that she had absolutely no interest in Cal. Rachael was sharp on her feet, frequently spraying Lara with flakes as she banked to kill the speed she would quickly gather. Lara felt inadequate in every way beside her. Rachael's spirits were buoyant. "What do you think we should wear tonight, Lara? Should we" — with a nasty grin — "wear anything?" As they boarded the lifts, she rattled off a string of dirty jokes. Trying to catch her breath and only half listening, Lara didn't get most of them. Two more runs and their separation from Mindy and Dana was complete. Finally, barely able to stand at the top of the hill, Lara suggested that they call it a day.

"Okay," Rachael said. "But let's go through the trees this time. I'm tired of this easy slide. Think you can handle it?"

"Sure," Lara said, dreading the prospect. The trees would have taxed the limits of her skill if she was fresh. And now, exhausted, she would be risking her neck; nevertheless, it was better than admitting to Rachael that she was afraid.

Rachael surprised her by shadowing her cautious pace. Maybe she was exhausted, too, Lara thought, for she had also fallen strangely silent. They maneuvered like a linked pair, giving each pine a wide berth, until they entered the most obstructed part of the course. Here Rachael began to press her right. Lara muttered for her to back off. Rachael was quick to oblige.

Lara was eyeing a cluster of approaching trees, plotting a strategy of turns, when Rachael suddenly accelerated, cutting directly across her path. She tried to brake, but the abruptness of the effort caused her to lose balance. It was as though a meaty football tackle had slammed the back of her knees. The desolate sky, the coated trees, the powdery snow, all blurred in a spinning collage. She was a snowball, and she wasn't slowing down. Way back in her head she remembered Percy's line about rolling to the bottom of the mountain. She wasn't anywhere near that lucky.

Lara heard rather than felt the impact, a thousand splintering wooden matches. Then there was silence. Her thoughts were a dreamy jumble. In retrospect, she realized that she had been only partially conscious, but her thoughts still held the common threat of absolute disgust for Rachael. That it had been an accident did not even cross her mind, for where was she? Lara opened her eyes, which took their time focusing. The clouds were calling her name, using Percy's voice. That must mean that she had damaged her brain, she thought. Poor girl will never be the same. Then the clouds squeezed her hand, and she knew that was impossible, even for crossed neurons.

"Lara," Percy was saying. "You're okay. Don't move."

He was contradicting himself, she thought. But she was so glad that he had come to her rescue, she ignored his advice and sat up. The landscape did a quick dance before settling down and letting her know she was entangled in a sharp-branched bush. Another foot and her skull would have smacked an ungiving thick trunk. Percy was kneeling by her side, concern darkening his handsome face.

She smiled. "Fancy meeting you here."

"Remain perfectly still. You may have a bone broken."

"I feel fine, really. Not a scratch." She wiped at a funny itch in her hair. When she drew her hand away, it was stained with blood. "Well, maybe a scratch," she muttered, flexing her arms and legs slowly. The damage appeared superficial. Ignoring Percy's protests, she tried to stand. Her left knee groaned, but that was the worst of it. "See, all in one piece," she said, untangling her pants with Percy's help.

He shook his head. "You were lucky. When I saw you lose your balance in front of these trees, I braced myself for the worst."

That he'd had such concern for her eased the pain she was beginning to feel from her cut. But the joy at seeing him was somewhat spoiled by the thought of Rachael's deed. "I didn't lose my balance. Rachael cut me off."

He was puzzled by her tone. "That happens, you hit ice and suddenly gain speed. I'm sure she didn't force you into these bushes on purpose."

Lara shut a *You don't know her the way I know her* in her mouth, and said instead, "Where is she?"

Percy's change of expression indicated that he was considering her accusation. "That wasn't very nice, leaving you here."

"Were you just passing by?" she asked, thinking, *Were you following me, thinking of me all day, mad to see me?*

He laughed. "No, I was following you."

"Really?" she beamed, then remembered that she had to be cool.

"I saw you get off the lift with Rachael. I was trying to catch up. I called several times but you mustn't have heard." He pulled back her hair near her cut. "That's still bleeding. Looks like it could use a few stitches."

"No way. Those doctors would want to cut my hair in the process." She added quietly, "Why were you following us?"

He spoke seriously. "To tell you we won't be coming tonight. I talked to Cal — that bastard — and he told me about his run-in with Dana. His was no doubt a distorted version, but I can guess the truth. I'd been having second thoughts anyway. Rachael didn't look too excited about having us over. Life's complicated enough. Why don't we just forget it."

"No," Lara said firmly. *Fool*, she told herself, *just give him your number*. But that would be too easy. And suddenly she was confident she could win Percy's affection, and she wanted Rachael there to rub her nose in it. God, Dana was right, this was a contest. "I've spoken with Dana," she exaggerated. "I think she likes Cal more than she — more than she gave him the impression she did. Just think, six girls trapped in a house together. We'll be so bored! Come, and don't worry about it. Please?"

Percy was unconvinced. "I don't know. You're the one who said she ran you into these trees. Maybe the party was the reason."

She shook off her skis as they started slowly toward the lodge. "If she did do it on purpose," she said boldly, "then I'll need you there to protect me."

Lara resisted all of Percy's attempts to have her see a doctor. By the time they had reached the ski lodge, her cut had dried and she felt all she needed was a good shampoo. However, her knee was throbbing. Only with difficulty had she disguised her limp from Percy. Boys liked tough girls, so she had heard.

On the same couch where she had waited

with Dana for Rachael and Mindy, they sat and chatted about snow and skiing. The colored parkas had thinned, most people calling it a day — which reminded Lara, where were the girls? Already the sun had gone behind the mountain. Probably they had started back without her. She was debating whether to call Nell when Percy mentioned that he'd like to get in more skiing.

"Isn't it too late?" Her euphoria was suddenly compromised. He wanted to ski when he could talk to her. He didn't love her. "I thought maybe we could have a bite to eat at the coffee shop."

He stood, already on his way, enough time wasted on her. "I never exercise on a full stomach," he said with his usual degree of charm. "Now, are you sure you're well enough to walk back to the house? It's a long way. I could tell you were limping and trying to hide it."

She didn't want to use that to keep him. "I feel a hundred percent better." She got up, trying not to wince with pain.

"You sure?"

"Positive."

He was in a hurry. "Catch you later, then. Between seven and eight is good?"

"Positive. I mean, perfect. Have a good time!"

An awkward hesitation followed, where they both stared at each other and fidgeted. She was hoping for a kiss. But he only patted her shoulder, told her to take care, and was gone. Feeling what she recognized as unfounded loneliness, she sat back down. The long hike on her stiff knee weighed on her mind.

At that moment, the ranger who had taken the keys to Dana's car was walking across the lobby toward the bar. "Sir?" she called. "Sir, did you bring our car down?"

He walked over to her with seeming reluctance. He was not wearing a uniform. He glanced at her bloody hair, smoothed his moustache nervously, and said, "Scratched your head, I see. Were you attacked by a bear?"

"A tree. I was wondering about our car."

He rummaged through his pockets, coming up empty-handed. He smiled, showing he needed dental work. "Must have left them in the office."

"Could we get them now?"

"I suppose so," he said, without a shred of enthusiasm. "Off duty now. You girls are staying till Sunday evening, ain't ya?"

"Yes."

"I'll have those keys waiting for you when you leave."

"I'd like to pick them up now."

"But the colonel was just going to enjoy watching a football game in the bar here. Look, they'll be here and sparkling and waitin' when you're ready to leave." He grinned again, more out of habit, it seemed, than out of warmth. He slapped her side roughly. "Watch out for them bears, you hear? They'll eat ya alive."

Before she could protest, he walked away. Suspicion dominated her thoughts. He had gone to the trouble of moving their cars and now couldn't be bothered returning their keys. Initially he'd worn no badge and now he was out of uniform. He seemed old for a ranger. Maybe he wasn't one, but a car thief instead. She would have to check that guy out.

Lara limped to the phone and searched her pockets for the number to Nell's house. It was gone; must have fallen out when she crashed. No matter, her memory was excellent, and she dialed what she was almost positive were the correct digits. But the phone on the other end rang and rang. That was odd, for even if Nell had gone for a walk, Celeste would not have been able to.

Her meager lunch in combination with the hours of strenuous exercise made her stomach grumble for attention. Ignoring her solemn vows to diet seven pounds away, she took a seat at the counter of the coffee shop and ordered a turkey sandwich, french fries, milk, and a huge slice of the chocolate cake Dana had eaten earlier. Nothing like a stuffed belly to uplift one's mood. She was asking for the bill when a rough voice intruded beside her.

"I hope you're more friendly than your partner."

It was Cal, crushing the adjacent stool, stinking of sweat, blowing hot breath in her face. "I hear the two of you didn't hit it off," she said carefully.

He leaned on the counter with his elbow, shoving a plate aside. "What did she tell you?" he demanded.

Lara shrugged. "Don't remember exactly. Coming to the party tonight?"

"Huh?"

Later, she would have to ask Dana's forgiveness for the liberties she was going to take with her name. "We're having a party at my friend's house tonight. Percy might have told you it was off but I talked him back into it. You're welcome to come. Give Dana another chance. She didn't sound that mad at you. To tell you the truth, she likes aggressive men."

Cal was perplexed, more so than her information could justify. His eyes lost their focus, as though he were thinking intently. "Percy told me about no party," he said finally.

"Doesn't matter. I'm telling you."

"Where is that guy, anyway? He told me he was coming to talk to you."

"He left about thirty minutes ago. He wanted to ski some more."

Cal nodded to himself, swinging his feet

onto the floor. "What did he tell you about me?" he asked warily.

"Percy? Not much. That you work together, live in the same place." Lara forced a chuckle. "Is there something I should know?"

"No."

She stuttered. "I was merely joking."

He smiled, patting her back with a heavy hand. "You girls fix us up a nice party. If you by chance see Dana, tell her I'm coming."

"Of course, I'll see her. I'm heading back now."

"Sure, yeah," he told the floor.

"Have *you* seen her?"

"Nooh. Hey, I've gotta split."

"Do you want directions in case you don't see Percy?"

"I know where the place is. Catch you later."

"Good-bye." Lara watched him leave. How did he know where Nell's house was if he'd never been there?

Chapter 3

The clouds had decided to give up their cargo. Stretching her head back and opening her mouth wide, Lara tried to catch snowflakes on her thirsty tongue. Despite a significant drop in temperature and a strengthening wind, she was hot and sweaty. Ages had elapsed since she had left the lodge and she was still nowhere near halfway home. Her knee no longer hurt so much as it refused to cooperate. The joint was mushy. Also, the grooves they had cut in the path on their way down were filling in. Whenever she skipped out of them, her cross-country skis sank an additional foot. All this work for a trifle of sensation; it was hardly worth the bother. If not for Percy, Lara decided, she would have given the day a failing grade.

Lara was leaning against a tree, taking a brief time-out, when she saw a figure approaching swiftly on skis from up the path. It was Mindy, obviously out of control and about to . . . thank God, she had sat down and stopped herself. Lara limped to her side and offered her hand.

"You don't belong in the fast lane," she said.

"Oh, it's you, Lara." Mindy retrieved her bubble gum from the snow and popped it back in her mouth. One of these days Mindy was going to bite her tongue off. Lara helped her up.

"You're going the wrong way. Where are the others?"

"I don't know where Rachael is. I haven't seen her since you two took off together. Dana's farther up the path. We were returning to the house when I decided I had better find you. What happened to your head?"

"The ranger said it was a bear. Now that you've found me, let's get home. This storm's getting nastier every minute."

Mindy looked unhappy. "I think I should try to find Rachael."

"How do you know she isn't ahead of you two?"

"Well, I don't. How do you know she is?"

"You were returning to the lodge to find Cal, right?"

"Nooo."

"Get off it, Mindy."

She was suddenly defensive. "What's so wrong with wanting to talk to him? I don't care what Dana says, I think he's a gentleman."

"I spoke to him just before I left. He's coming tonight to the party. You don't have to go to the lodge."

"I still want to."

"You're not. You should never have left Dana. She's a bigger clod than you. What if she trips and sprains her ankle and has no one to help her? Come, we're going home."

"Why should I?" But there was no authority in her voice.

"Because I am telling you."

"But I'd like to see him."

Lara softened. "You will, tonight. Besides, I've hurt my knee and I'm not feeling very strong. What do you say, pal?"

"Okay." Mindy squinted. "You really ran into a bear?"

Lara laughed. "One you know all too well."

They were three quarters of an hour farther along — it took a lot longer going up than going down — when they came across a most mysterious find. *One* of Dana's skis lay half covered in the tracks. Scattered footsteps led away from it approximately ten yards up the path, disappearing in a concave impression that looked uncannily familiar. Beyond the impression, there were no footsteps.

"What the hell," Mindy muttered, sliding forward to investigate. Lara stopped her.

"Stay here."

"What's wrong?"

"Don't disturb the evidence."

Mindy was suddenly frightened. "You think we're in danger?"

Lara shook her head. "I don't know what to think." She crept forward cautiously, squatting by the ski. If it were broken, that might have given Dana reason to leave it. She tested the spring-pressured clasps that fastened onto the boots. One had lost its elasticity, but then, hadn't Dana mentioned that earlier, that it had always been that way? These Olin skis cost a bundle, to simply discard. And then there was the impression in the snow. Of course, she had seen the same phenomenon where the vanishing snowman had been. Lara moved up the path and knelt, poking a finger through the inch of fresh snow that was filling the crater. It was hard, ice. She brushed clear a patch. The frozen sheet was flaked with dirty gray.

"Lara?" Mindy called, her panic rising. "What is it?"

As though the snowman had suddenly caught fire.

Without two skis, Dana would have littered the path with footsteps. There were no footsteps. It was as though Dana had reached this spot and gone neither forward or backward. She had simply stopped and vanished. What had stopped her? Where could she have gone? The Bermuda Triangle didn't reach this far west.

Lara broke two branches from a nearby bush and, using the string that tightened her jacket hood, fastened an awkward cross to an adjacent tree. If necessary, she would be able to find this exact spot. Returning to a trembling Mindy, she asked, "Where were the two of you on the path when you split up?"

"I don't know. We were near here. Oh, God, do you think something's happened to her?"

"How far would you say we are from the house?"

Mindy pointed vaguely. "We just have to wrap around these trees. Fifteen minutes, maybe twenty. Why would Dana leave her ski in the snow?"

"It won't have been the first weird thing that Dana's done," Lara said. This reassured Mindy. Obviously she did not notice all the inconsistencies in the situation. Lara picked up the ski. It was cold, naturally. Yet the chill that caused her to shiver was from foreboding. "Let's get out of this place," she said suddenly.

Shortly afterward, they rounded a bend and saw the house with a warming scent and trail of smoke rising from the chimney. Nell was sitting on the porch steps, her head resting in her clasped hands on propped-up elbows. She did not notice them. Only when Mindy called, did she look up.

"Have a good time?" she asked, glancing at the extra ski Lara carried.

"Okay," Lara said. "Rach here?"

"Haven't seen her."

Lara dropped Dana's ski. "Seen Dana?"

"Yeah."

Her flood of relief made her realize how worried she'd been. "How long ago did she get back?"

"Didn't you see her on the way up? I mean, she's not here. I saw her way down on the path about an hour ago before she went behind the trees. In fact, I was beginning to worry about her. I figured that she had stopped and was taking a rest, but then she was taking so long to reappear. I was about to ski down, when I saw you two coming up. Dana should know better than to ski off the path."

"She didn't," Lara said, the lump reforming in her stomach. "This is her ski. We found it on the path, just this one."

Nell heard her concern. "She couldn't have just disappeared."

"The snowman did," Lara whispered, more to herself. Quickly she gave Nell the details of the abandoned ski and the impression in the snow. She concluded by asking, "Is there another path down to the lodge that intersects this one?"

"Not really," Nell said. "Though, if enough people ski through a place it can be just as good as a path. That's probably what happened. She probably took off on some tangent."

"Why would she do that?" Mindy asked.

"Maybe she wanted to circle back to the lodge," Nell said, checking out the darkening clouds. It was difficult to be sure, but the sun had probably set. "A little late for that."

"I don't think so," Lara muttered.

Mindy came to life, in a foul mood. "That's it! That's what she did! She knew I was going back to see Cal and she wanted to get there first. She snuck off the path trying to find a shortcut."

"And left one of her skis?" Lara asked, irritated. "Don't be ridiculous. Besides, there were no tracks except the ski grooves."

"You're right," Nell said, thoughtful. "The only logical explanation is that Dana left the path well before you found this ski, and that this ski is not really hers. Olin — it's a common brand."

"I could swear it's hers," Lara said, now not altogether certain. There still remained the question of how someone else left it without making tracks. "Yet, you must be right."

"She's stealing him away from me!" Mindy complained. "Why can't she find her own guys! Cal was supposed to be mine!"

Nell chuckled. "Who's this Cal? Is he one of the guys coming to the party?"

Lara decided to let matters rest for the time being. Nell's explanation had not erased the mystery, but surely there was a harmless, logical explanation. Plus Nell's own change in mood was supportive. Her initial gloom seemed to have dissolved. Yet Lara knew only too well how quickly that could change. "Yes, he is," she said. "Boy, have I got a story for you."

"That conniving bitch," Mindy grumbled.

"Have you got a guy for me?" Nell asked.

"I'm afraid those are in short supply for this party," Lara said. "So far, only two are coming. I forgot to ask, how are you feeling?"

"Fine, I just needed a rest."

"How's Celeste?" Lara asked.

Nell paused. An unreadable emotion flicked across her face. "She's in the shower."

Not that that answered the question. "You two have a lot to talk about?"

Nell was hardly listening. "She seems a nice girl."

Lara left them on the porch. The house had so many rooms, she had to search for the bathroom where Celeste was taking her shower. Behind one door, the light was on. Knocking lightly, she went inside.

"Celeste?"

Through the hot steam, as if she had suddenly been cornered by Jack the Ripper, Celeste jumped behind the opaque shower curtain and wrapped it about her naked body. The water was off; she had been drying. Lara chuckled at her modesty, saying, "I didn't mean to startle you."

Well hidden, Celeste breathed, "That's okay. How was the skiing?"

"Great. Met this guy. Have to tell you all

about him when you're done. What have you and Nell been up to?"

"What do you mean?"

"Nothing specific. What have you done since I saw you last?"

"Nothing. We talked."

"About what?"

"Things."

The reaction was similar to Nell's. If anything, Celeste sounded vaguely angry. She had never seen Celeste angry before. She wouldn't have thought it possible. "Do you like her?"

Celeste had wrapped herself in a towel, still behind the curtain, obviously waiting for her to leave to continue drying. "Who?" she asked.

"Why, Nell."

"She seems a nice girl."

Like an echo. "You heard about the party," Lara said, beginning to leave. "When you're dressed, come to the kitchen. Maybe our two heads together can whip up something eatable."

Celeste's voice was enthusiastic. "I'm really glad we're having a party."

"Is Nell using the adjacent bedroom?" Lara asked idly. On the sink counter was a jar of prescription skin cream for an *N. Kutroff*. Probably Nell still had to treat the areas that had been grafted.

"I don't know."

"She must be. Me, I would have taken the master bedroom. Anyway, start drumming up your best recipes."

"I love cooking."

"Great. Hey, Nell hasn't left the house at any time, has she?"

"No."

"That's good."

The crackling fire in the living room was seductive. Lara took a minute to sit on the surrounding bricks, letting the warmth ease her tired muscles. Nell had piled high the logs. One would have thought she would have been wary of fires.

"What happened to you?" Rachael's voice rang.

Lara cautioned herself to be cool. "I ran into a tree."

"You ran into a tree," Rachael repeated, not taking her answer seriously. "What happened to your head?"

Lara had forgotten the dried blood. She would have to take a shower immediately. Curious how Nell hadn't commented on it. "Actually, it was a bush I ran into. Didn't you know?"

Rachael was either a master liar or else she was innocent.

"You're saying that when you suddenly dropped behind, you had run into a tree?"

"A bush. A sharp one. Ruined my jacket."

"You poor dear. I didn't know. I looked and suddenly you were gone. Are you hurt?"

"No."

"Better wash that blood out of your hair. It looks totally gross."

Lara toyed with the idea of harping on how Percy had come to her rescue. Better to have Percy bring it up, she decided. "Have you seen Dana?"

Rachael snickered. "Nell and Mindy asked me about her. No, I haven't. Bet she's back at the lodge. Nothing she likes better than a good feel and Cal's perfect for that, though that's probably all he's good for."

"Where have you been all this time?"

"Skiing."

"This entire time?"

"Hey, what is this? If I was making out with Percy, I don't gotta tell you."

"You couldn't have been doing that."

"Sure about that, Princess Lara?"

Lara smiled sweetly. "Couldn't have been kissing two girls at the same time, could he, Princess Rachael?" Before she could respond, Lara left the room. But not before she saw Rachael's flawless jaw drop heavily. She'd won that round. Still, the final score was all that mattered.

In the kitchen, before taking an inventory of Nell's stock, Lara called the lodge. The number was on a typed sheet posted next to the phone.

"Park Administration. Can I help you?"

"Yes, my name is Lara Johnson. I'm up from Oakland with friends for the weekend.

We're staying at the Kutroff residence in the Cedar Stream area. The problem is — actually, I'm not sure if it is a problem — is that my girl friend has sort of disappeared. Her name is Dana Miller."

He was brisk. "How has she 'sort of disappeared'?"

"We don't know where she is."

"When and where was the last time you saw her?"

"Another girl friend of mine was with her an hour and a half, maybe two hours ago. They split up on the path that leads from the lodge to Cedar Stream. We assumed she was walking home alone ahead of us. We found one of her skis — at least, I think it's hers — on the trail. You know where I mean?"

"Yes." He seemed to be taking notes. "You're not sure it was her ski?"

"Not positive." Lara realized how nebulous she was being. "Look, perhaps she'll show up soon. It's still early. I guess what I really want to know is if she has returned to the lodge, can she leave a message with you that would get to me?"

"Certainly. What is your number?" Lara gave it to him off the phone, identical to the number she had called earlier and gotten no answer to. "Got it."

"Good. Is the storm still on for tonight?" If Percy wasn't able to come, she might not have a chance to give him her number. She might not see him again.

"Definitely. Should be a beaut. Miss, if that's all —"

"One other thing. Do you have a ranger on staff who looks like Colonel Sanders?"

"Pardon me?"

"The chicken guy. A ranger who looks like and calls himself the colonel said he was going to move our cars for us. I was wondering if he was legit."

"I know of no one on our staff who fits that description. But then again, I am new here. Did he take your keys?"

"Yes he did."

"Then you might have a problem. I'll check into it at this end. And I'll page Dana Miller periodically until she shows up. Contact me if she returns home."

"Who should I ask for?"

"Roger McCormick. I'll be at the desk all night."

"Thank you, Roger." Putting down the phone, Lara was more worried about Dana's car than Dana herself. And the colonel had moved Rachael's BMW also. Well, there was nothing she could do about it now.

Food for the party would have to be the priority. She was pleased to discover that Nell had stocked a diverse supply of sandwich ingredients: rye and wheat bread, cold cuts, french rolls, cheese, lettuce, butter, tomatoes, plus bags of chips and cartons of dips, and an entire case of Coke. That would take care of dinner, but dessert would have to have a personal touch. She was flipping through a ten-pound cookbook, thinking that she would never be able to bake anything that even remotely resembled the luscious color photos, when Celeste came to her rescue.

Celeste was not merely a good cook, she was a certified chef. "Cold cuts," she asked in amazement, "and you like this boy?" She installed Lara in the corner out of the way, grating lemons for a meringue pie, while she prepared two chickens, clothing them in a concoction of herbs that Lara had always assumed people had in their kitchens for looks. That was but the beginning. Soon Celeste had the entire contents of the cupboards arranged on the table and counter top, moving each ingredient toward an invisible feast.

Casually she inquired about Percy. Lara needed little encouragement to pour out her heart. "Oh, he's the cutest, I mean absolutely the best-looking guy that I've ever. . . ." The other girls were working to give the house a festive atmosphere, wandering in and out of the kitchen only to stuff food in their mouths. Rachael strolled in while Lara was describing Percy's voice. More harsh nonverbal exchanges. Lara was getting used to them. But she was afraid that Nell would be upset at the control Celeste had taken of her kitchen. Yet Nell seemed to take it all in stride.

With her pie tucked in the oven, Lara left Celeste to take a shower and wash the blood out of her hair. The cut reopened and the red drops trailing down her naked body made her feel slightly dizzy. There was no way she could bandage it. The hot water also made her drowsy and a nap sounded just perfect. But before she lay down on her bed, she gave the house a white-glove inspection. Was she expecting to find Dana tucked away in a secret hideout in Cal's arms? Not really, but she had a nagging compulsion that bid her search till she could find *something*.

The house was massive, and there were many empty rooms in which if she stood perfectly still she could hear the sighing of the timbers as they buffeted the rising wind. The end of the search found her in the basement, beside a snowmobile and the huge, recently installed propane tank that Nell had mentioned, cold to her hesitant touch. It was scary. The image of a shattered house rising on a mushroom cloud formed and lingered in her mind. Why these constant thoughts about fire? Unseen flames seemed ready to spark out of the air.

She was drawn outside a side door to study again the impression marking the snowman's disappearance. But drifts created by the storm had erased the concave dish of ice. Nevertheless, she went down on her hands and knees, feeling for the spot, numbing her exposed fingers, freezing her damp hair, eventually giving up and staggering out of the dark back into the house to her bedroom.

Thawing out beneath layers of blankets, *colorless* fire sparkled inside her closed eyes. There was a face inside the flames, a face that should have slipped into the past, but that continued to shadow her, haunt her — a melting face in horrifying pain. . . .

Chapter 4

"Why do I always have to baby-sit her?" Nell complained to her mother.

"Because she's your little sister," Mrs. Kutroff said, pulling the long Cadillac into Dana's driveway. "You should be happy you have one."

"I'd rather have a little brother who played with trucks all by himself," Nell said.

"Hush, now. We're here." Mrs. Kutroff turned to the backseat. "Have all your things?"

"Yes, Mrs. Kutroff," Lara said politely, hugging her pillow and blanket to her chest.

"Mommy, I forgot my toothbrush!" Nicole exclaimed, terribly worried.

"Moron," Nell muttered.

"You can share your sister's," Mrs. Kutroff said.

"No way!" Nell shouted, shaking her head. "Uh! Uh!"

"Nell!" Mrs. Kutroff said.

"You can use mine, Nicole," Lara said, happy Nicole was to be part of their slumber party. Nicole was fun. Actually, she was more fun than Nell. Nicole smiled and thanked her.

Rachael and Mindy were already inside. Mindy had accidently squished a piece of used bubble gum on the couch, and Dana was trying to get it off before her parents — who were watching TV upstairs — found out. Rachael was eating cake and ice cream, and drinking a can of Coke. She ate like a pig and never got fat. Lara knew that Rachael would be beautiful when she grew up. So would Nicole.

It was already getting dark so they stayed inside and watched a rented movie on a fancy projector. Nell's parents had brought over the projector earlier. They were rich; there was nothing that Nell and Nicole didn't get. The show was Doctor Zhivago, and all of them agreed that Omar Sharif had the most beautiful eyes in the whole world. Though Rachael said he wasn't such a hot guy. When he visited Julie Christie in town, she said that he was actually having sex with her. Rachael was sure of this although Lara did not think he would do such a thing. But she didn't argue with Rachael. From listening to her talk before, it seemed Rachael really did know a lot about sex and who was doing it.

After the movie, they broke into two teams and played charades. Nicole was on Dana's and her side because Nell was still mad at her sister for having come. Too bad for their team. Nicole was better at charades than all of them put together. She seemed able to place the mystery word directly in their minds. Nell even accused her of cheating, she was so good.

Dana's father came in and said that he was going to bed. He didn't want them making a lot of noise or staying up late. After he left, Rachael said wickedly, "Now we can have some real fun."

"Do you have a boy coming over?" Dana asked, excited. Already she liked boys. Lara didn't know what she liked about them.

"No, silly." Rachael went to the bar and picked up a crystal decanter filled with dark red liquid. Lara thought it looked like dirty blood. Rachael took a gulp.

"Don't!" Dana screamed. "My dad will know. He'll kill me!"

"Shh!" Rachael said sternly. "We can put some water in the bottles. He'll never know. Trust me, my brother taught me this trick."

"I don't like alcohol," Lara said.

"That's because you've never been drunk," Rachael said, uncapping a second bottle and sniffing the contents.

"What's drunk?" Nicole asked, joining Rachael and smelling the bottles, too.

"Don't you know anything?" Nell said. "Drunk is when you have a hangover and you can't drive and your head hurts."

"My head has never hurt," Rachael disagreed, dropping ice cubes into a row of glasses. "Drunk is when you feel good and laugh a lot. We're all going to get drunk right now."

Lara hated the taste of the brandy that Rachael gave her — it was like swallowing gasoline — but she drank it all quickly and asked for more, not wanting to seem like a sissy. They stole from a variety of colored bottles. Rachael was right about one thing: they did start to laugh a lot. Nicole threw up once but said she felt fine afterward.

Lara began to get bored and rather dizzy. She suggested that they play another game. Trouble was, nobody could think of one.

"In this movie I saw they jumped over candles," Dana said.

"And?" Rachael asked.

"I dunno the rest," she muttered, finishing her drink and belching. "I don't feel much like jumping, anyway."

"Let's play Monopoly," Lara said.

"Rex chewed up Marvin Gardens," Dana said. "Can't."

"Candles, candles," Rachael whispered to herself. Suddenly her eyes flashed in her unusually red face. "I've got it! Let's have a séance! Dana, I remember seeing a Ouija board in your bedroom. You get it, and we'll turn off the lights and light some candles and incense and talk to the spirits."

"What spirits would want to talk to six drunk girls?" Lara said, slurring her words.

"Get the board, Dana," Rachael said, ignoring her.

Their gypsy parlor took only a few minutes to prepare. Mindy and Nell cleaned off the coffee table and draped it with a sheet. Dana fetched Parker Brothers' standard brown rectangular divining board and wiped clear the dust. Rachael jammed long white candles in silver candleholders — courtesy of the china cabinet — and arranged them in a precarious circle around the board. Nell told Nicole that she was too young to help move the planchette. Lara muttered that she didn't want to move the planchette. Rachael gave her a pen and paper, and told her to take notes. Because of the poor light, Lara took a seat at the bar where there was a fold-down red pocket light. Looking rejected, Nicole sat on the floor at her feet.

"What should we ask?" Mindy said, as the four of them placed their fingers on the plastic indicator.

"I'll do the questioning," Rachael said. "Nell, lighten your touch."

"Sure."

"Who's there?" Rachael asked.

The spirits could have been asleep. Lara chuckled. Rachael told her to shut up, give it time. Minutes dragged by. Finally the indicator began to move, in small ellipses that slowly grew to where the planchette was swinging between YES and NO.

"Who's there?" Rachael repeated. "Here

it goes! U ... getting this, Lara? U ... S ... us."

"I could have told you that," Lara muttered.

"Hey, you moving this thing, Rach?" Dana asked.

"No."

"Then you're moving it, Mindy," Dana said. "Somebody's moving it."

"I ain't," Mindy said. "You aren't, are you, Nell?"

"We all are," Rachael said. "Our subconscious is." She spoke to the board. "Isn't that right?"

The planchette swung to YES.

"See," Rachael said.

"I'm going to ask something," Mindy said. "Will I get a B in math?"

The indicator went to F. Everyone, except Mindy, laughed.

"You moved it to that!" Mindy accused Dana.

"I did not!"

"Well I'm getting at least a C in math. I don't care what it says."

"Then why did you ask?" Rachael asked, annoyed. "I told you, I'll do the questioning." She cleared her throat. "Am I going to be a rich and famous actress when I grow up?" YES, *was the answer. "See, it's working," Rachael told Mindy.*

Rachael inquired after all of their futures. Dana was going to have six children and be

66

plump all her life. Mindy was going to visit a foreign country and work in a factory until she retired. Lara was going to be an international journalist who married four times. Nell was going to write the greatest mystery novel of all time. Only for Nicole did it give no hint of the future. This depressed the young girl. Lara patted her head and told her not to worry.

"We should get serious," Rachael said finally. "Let's try to find out how this thing really works." She put on her official voice. "Are there any spirits in this room?"

YES

"How many?"

SIX.

"Six of us, six spirits," Lara said.

"Are we the six spirits?" Rachael asked.

It swung between YES *and* NO, *finally settling on* NO.

"Ask if Captain Howdy's here," Mindy said, afraid.

"Who?"

"The demon in The Exorcist *who made the little girl barf up her guts," Mindy said.*

"Is Captain Howdy here?" Rachael asked.

NO

"Are there any evil spirits in the room?" Nell asked.

YES

"Really?" Rachael asked, frowning.

YES

"Are we in danger?"

"Who is the evil spirit?" Rachael asked. Something seemed to be distracting her. As she spelled out the letters, her voice was strained. *"N — I — C — O — L — E. Nicole,"* Rachael whispered, all eyes focusing on the young girl, whose lips quivered and hands trembled.

"This is dumb," Dana said, backing away from the board.

"Let's quit," Lara said, rubbing Nicole's shoulders.

"Did it really spell out my name?" Nicole asked, crawling toward the Ouija board on her knees, tears in her voice.

"Yet, but —" Rachael began, considering.

"But what?" Nell asked.

Rachael scratched her head, and spoke to Nicole. *"Look, it's just a toy. It doesn't mean anything."*

"Ask again, please?" Nicole said, wiping damp cheeks.

Rachael looked to Nell, who shrugged. Mindy nodded, placing her fingers back on the planchette. Dana shook her head and stepped away from the table. *"Couldn't hurt,"* Rachael said.

"Sure could," Lara whispered.

"Who's the evil spirit in the room?" Rachael asked.

The planchette did not spell. It revolved until the sharp end was pointing at Nicole. Again Rachael frowned, seemingly on the verge of complaining. Mindy whistled. Nell chuckled. Nicole burst into tears.

"Nicole —" Lara began.

"I hate this!" Nicole cried, leaping to her feet, swatting the indicator away. Unfortunately, in doing so, her hand accidentally hooked onto the base of a double candleholder and dragged it toward her, off the table and onto the carpet. Maybe because they were all slightly drunk, no one reacted immediately. Nicole's eyes widened with terrific surprise, and perhaps for an instant one could have thought she looked evil. Orange light played on her face. Smoke rose through her hair, a noise crackled at her feet, the stink of something burning filled the air.

"The carpet!" Dana said. "My parents will kill —"

"Why you little snot!" Nell cursed, preparing to slap Nicole.

"For God's sake, put it out!" Rachael said, searching for something to smother the fire with.

What happened next did not appear to take place in normal time. There were frantic rushes where all of them sought to help and only made matters worse, laced with horrific pauses where they froze and begged inside for things to pass.

Nell struck Nicole in the face, forcing her back. Dana and Mindy grabbed folded magazines and banged at the burning carpet. Rachael yanked a cushion from the sofa in the event the magazines failed. Lara pulled the top from the decanter of brandy, poised to drown the fire.

Nicole began to scream. Her robe was on fire.

Nicole stood with her back to Lara, the flames climbing up her front. Still, Lara could see the quivering glow as it fanned from Nicole's sides like a deadly aura. Nell squatted at her sister's feet, her mouth transfixed with amazement and fear. Dana and Mindy buried their faces in their hands.

"Roll on the floor!" Rachael shouted, dropping the cushion and ripping at the sheet that covered the coffee table. Ouija board and candles went flying. Simultaneously, Nell sprang and grabbed Nicole by the pink wool sweater the young girl was wearing over her polyester yellow robe, throwing her to the floor. Giving no thought to the flames that began to burn her, Nell tried to suffocate the fire. The fire was losing, and surely would have been extinguished by Rachael's sheet, when Lara forgot that she was holding hard liquor and not wine. Because it was wet, she poured the entire decanter over Nicole's lower body. And it was strange how the sudden drenching seemed to work. For an instant the fire disappeared. Nell even stopped rolling Nicole and pulled back her hands. Rachael dropped her sheet. Dana and Mindy breathed sighs of relief. Lara smiled and smelled the empty bottle.

Then Nicole exploded like a Molotov cocktail.

Fearless, Nell reached forward to pull her sister from the blaze. At once her hair disintegrated, her face lost in a closing hand of black smoke. She did not seem to feel pain or think of the consequences. Mindy fainted like a crumpling paper doll. Dana rammed both her fists into her eyes and began to gag. Nicole's screams cut off like a power failure, sending a permanent darkness into Lara's heart. Nicole lay still, no longer writhing. Lara stared at the empty bottle in her hand and thought of her terrible mistake.

"Out of the way!" Rachael ordered. Picking up the sheet, she seized Nell by the nape of the neck and dragged her aside. Spreading the white blanket between her two outstretched hands, she brought it down swiftly over Nicole. The fire went out. Immediately, before it could stick, Rachael removed the ruined linen. A putrid cloud of smoke choked the room. Lara's misty eyes were drawn downward. No, that couldn't be Nicole. She shook herself. Away, bad dream, let me wake up. But she couldn't wake up, because this was real.

Wearing only his underwear, Dana's father appeared. He knelt by Nicole, feeling for a pulse at the side of the neck, one of the few areas not scorched. Lying face down, Nicole did not flinch.

"Is she alive?" Rachael asked.

Mr. Miller shook his head. "I don't think so," he said, very pale.

"No," Lara whispered. "Not true, it can't be —"

"She's dead."

Lara did not know who said that. Her knees lost their strength, bringing her down to Nicole's side. She touched Nicole's left hand, amazingly cool and uninjured. A part of her desperately wanted to go into the girl to compensate for what she had done to her. "Nicole, Nicole," she chanted softly. "Please hear me."

And Nicole did stir, and did turn and look at her, with a single, bloodshot hazel eye. She had not heard the pronouncement clearly, but she had heard enough.

"I am going to die," Nicole said.

Lara squeezed her hand. "I will not let you die." It was a promise she swore she would keep. Even when Nicole's eye fell shut and did not open again.

Mrs. Miller called an ambulance. Ice packs were made up and Rachael held one to Nell's burns. Nell was catatonic, her features a blur of soft wax. Starch-white paramedics arrived. Normal time returned.

Nicole lived an entire week, until she was transferred from the local hospital to the UCLA Medical Center Burn Clinic. There she caught an infection and all the parents, including Mr. and Mrs. Kutroff, thought that it was probably for the best. She was buried in a large funeral in Oakland, and the mayor of the city came and said a few words. Thankfully, they left the coffin closed.

Nell was operated on immediately, given a series of skin grafts. The plastic surgeons felt that her face could be restored to a "reasonable degree." None of the girls visited her while she was in the hospital, or called her on the phone. Nell had told her mom and dad to tell them that she wanted never to see them again. Yet her parents blamed no one, and no lawsuits were filed. A month after the accident, the Kutroff family moved away.

Lara carried the blame alone, although accusing words were never spoken in her presence. She tried to talk to Dana, but Dana would just start to cry. Rachael took the philosophical point of view. There was no sense dwelling upon it. Fairly sophisticated for a ten-year-old, but of no comfort to Lara. Miraculously, Mindy had blanked the entire incident out of her mind. Occasionally she would even ask where Nicole was. Dead, Mindy. Oh, yeah. Lara's parents tried to help, but, not having been there, they couldn't understand and alleviate the pain the way the girls could have. Six months after the accident, she wasn't eating, and was fading into a wraith, unable to do schoolwork, unable to sleep without nightmares. Her parents took her to a child psychologist. He asked many questions. She gave few answers. The medicine he prescribed let her sleep but never *made her forget. Actually, matters had cleared in her own mind. Lara wanted to die because she had lied to Nicole by allowing her to die.*

It was at this time that Nell called. She wanted Lara to visit her for the weekend.

Lara was a pale sack of bones; nevertheless she was shocked at Nell's appearance. The initial skin grafts had focused more on replacing the skin than on what the skin looked like. Lara didn't even recognize her. However, Nell's spirits were excellent and more effective than a thousand hours of professional therapy. They talked late into the night. The incident was not dwelled upon, nor was it glossed over. Once Lara tried to apologize, but Nell made it clear that — in her own mind — it had been absolutely no one's fault. She added, "Now we can all be friends again."

Only once did they cry, reflecting on how beautiful Nicole would have been when she grew up.

Chapter 5

"Lara? Can you hear me? Wake up, Lara."

"Dirty blood!" she cried, bolting upright. Hands were on her shoulders.

"Lara!"

"Oh, God," she gasped. "Ashes in the coffin."

"Stop it!"

"Nicole, Nicole," she chanted. But the face in the fire began to fade replaced by an anxious Celeste, sitting beside her on the bed. The room was dark and warm, her T-shirt cooked with sweat, her heart thumping her rib cage. She had only been remembering. It was not happening again. "I was dreaming," she muttered in apology.

"About what?" Celeste asked, releasing her, easing back.

Lara wiped at her eyes, thankful for the poor light. She had been crying. "Nothing," she said quickly. "What time is it?"

"Close to seven. I thought I'd better wake you. Are you okay?"

"Perfect. Has Dana returned?"

"No."

Lara took a deep breath, trying to remain calm. She was far from perfect. "Has Park Administration called?"

"No one has."

They must have Dana's motives reversed. Probably she had returned to the lodge to avoid Cal. But why hadn't she called? "I guess the guys aren't here."

"No. The food is almost ready, though."

"You dear, I bet you've been working on it since I konked out." Feeling a sudden rush of love for Celeste, she leaned forward and hugged her. "I'm glad you're here," she said.

"Yeah?" Celeste said softly, slightly embarrassed, uncertain.

Lara sat back against the pillows. "Yeah, definitely." She smiled. "I hope we stay friends forever."

Celeste looked away. "I don't know."

"Sure we will. Even if I go away to school, we will write and talk on the phone."

"Where are you going?"

"I told you, Humboldt. Don't you remember? Of course, I still have to be accepted."

"What if you're accepted and you don't go?"

"Why wouldn't I go? Hey, what's wrong?"

Celeste was fidgeting, keeping her eyes averted. "I want to tell you something," she said slowly, with difficulty.

"What?"

"Oh, I don't know. It's nothing."

Lara moved closer. "Tell me."

"I don't like it here," she said suddenly.

"Why? Is it Nell?"

"No."

"What is it then?"

Celeste was searching for words. "I like the snow and trees. We saw a white rabbit disappear into a hole. But, I'm . . . I'm afraid."

"Of what?"

Celeste just shook her head.

"Maybe you're homesick. Why don't you call your aunt? Nell wouldn't mind."

"That wouldn't change. . . . I did."

"You called?"

"Yes." Celeste reached for her hand, changed her mind. "I really do like Nell."

"Good," Lara said, confident that she'd hit the nail on the head when she'd mentioned being homesick. Celeste had obviously led a sheltered life. This trip away from home was probably a first. Lara tugged at her damp T-shirt. "I better get dressed. Can't compete with Rachael in my underwear. Or maybe that's what it will take. Just kidding!"

Celeste stood reluctantly. "You're really looking forward to going away to school, aren't you?"

"Don't worry. It's only a five-hour drive. And I love to drive."

Celeste nodded. "I will check on the chickens."

"Be down in a sec to help you. And Celeste, if you want to go home a day earlier, just let me know."

Celeste left the room. Lara climbed out of bed and put on her unused pair of burgundy cords — cursing the fact that she hadn't brought a dress — and a flimsy pink shirt that needed both pockets, not to be indecent. She was brushing her hair when she decided to call the lodge again about Dana. Rather than go downstairs, she trekked up the hall looking for a phone in one of the other bedrooms. The door to one of the rooms was closed, muffled voices coming through the wood. Sounded like Rachael and Mindy. Lara was on the verge of knocking when she thought she heard her name mentioned. Naturally she put her ear to the door.

"We could get in serious trouble," Mindy was saying.

"Damn your whining, you coward. Who will there be to squeal?" Rachael snapped. She continued in a softer voice, obviously into a phone: "Don't worry, I'm behind you a hundred percent. Who cares about Dana? She's out of the way. Lara's the only one that matters. She's smart, but she'll never know, not until it's too late." Rachael chuckled. "Who could image such power! I can hardly believe it. Fate must have brought us together. . . . Hmm, let me think about it. . . . Get me what I want first and then we'll see. . . . No problem with the car. . . . To hell with her; she's just another fly to swat. . . ."

The blood roaring in Lara's ears made it difficult to hear. She had to know who Rachael was talking to, what they were talking about. The master bedroom would have another extension. Lara tiptoed away from the door and hopped up a short flight of stairs. The light to the room was out so she was surprised to find Nell kneeling on the floor, fighting with something stuck in the closet.

"Oh, sorry," Lara said, taking her hand off the thrown switch.

Nell sprang to her feet, her eyes wide, sliding the mirrored closet door shut at her back. "Christ, you startled me! Why are you here? . . . What can I do for you, Lara?"

"I'd like to use your phone."

"There are four phones downstairs," Nell said sharply.

She wanted Nell's phone because the ones downstairs could not be unplugged. If she simply picked up the receiver, no matter how carefully, Rachael would know. "I'm in a hurry," she said.

Anger, never too far from the surface of Nell's personality, flashed in her eyes. It remained even when she smiled thinly and said, "Suit yourself. I suppose you want privacy?"

Lara nodded.

"Sorry I snapped at you," Nell said, stepping by her.

"Thanks, Nell." Lara shut the door behind her. She unplugged the phone, picked up the receiver, then carefully fitted the metal prong back in the wall. Rachael was gabbing: "I never read the book, but I enjoyed the movie. It was wicked when she wasted everyone at the prom. Oh, so that's where you got this idea! Wait a sec. Don't say anything! I think there's someone else on the line. Hey, who's there?"

Lara thought fast. Hanging up would lead Rachael to suspect that her entire conversation had been overheard, probably stopping her from doing what she had planned. And Lara wanted to know what that plan was. Best to act as if she had just picked up the phone to make a call. She began to press the numbers like she was dialing. The high beeps would irritate —

"Stop that!!!" Rachael screamed.

"Are you using the phone?" Lara asked with brilliant innocence.

"No, I'm dusting the furniture and just happen to have it taped to my ear. Would you please get off the line and let me finish?"

"Will you be long?" She wanted to prolong the conversation. Just one word from the other party could tell her a great deal.

"No."

"How long?"

"Six-point-twenty-three minutes. How should I know, Lara? Get off the line!"

"Nell asked that we make no long-distance calls," she lied.

"This is not a long-distance call."

"Who do you know around here?"

"It's none of your business!"

Lara faked a sexy tone. "Hi there, are you someone I know?"

"Lara," Rachael said very quietly. "I already counted to ten. I am not counting to twenty. Put the goddamn phone down. Now!"

"You don't have to get angry," Lara said, finally complying. Rachael was up to no good and she had a male accomplice. But who was he, and how serious were their intentions? With Mindy involved it seemed impossible that it was anything *really* bad. But that line about Dana being out of the way, and Dana's disappearance, did not sit well. Lara was tempted to confront Rachael with what she'd heard, but the accusations sounded so ridiculous in her own mind that she decided to hold off.

Leaving the room, she found Nell standing immediately outside the door. Embarrassed, Nell said quickly, "I wanted to get my sweater."

"I see."

"Make your call?"

"No, Rachael's on the line."

"The phones downstairs are separate."

"Are they? That number you gave me —453–6672 — is that upstairs or downstairs?"

"Downstairs. Why?"

"Is that the right number? I called it from the lodge and no one answered."

"Yes, I spoke with you. Don't you remember?"

"No, I called a second time. I didn't have the slip of paper that you gave me, but I'm pretty sure that I dialed correctly. Did you and Celeste go out?"

"Only on the porch. Seems we would have heard one of the phones. You probably dialed wrong."

"What if you'd been in the basement?"

"I never go down there."

"I was down there."

"You were! Why?"

"Browsing around. What's the big deal? Is it dangerous?"

"My father doesn't want us fooling around down there because of the new propane tank."

Nell had had Rachael and Mindy cleaning the basement out. Couldn't be too dangerous. "I'll consider it off limits."

"I wish the stupid thing was buried outside somewhere."

"So you're sleeping in the master bedroom after all? I thought you were using the room adjacent to Celeste's."

"What made you think that?"

"I don't remember," she said honestly.

* * *

Lara spent the next hour making and applying four different colors of icing to a carrot cake that Celeste had baked. She drew a miserable carrot with two blurred nibbling bunnies. The passing minutes were fretful. Dana hadn't shown up, and the line to the lodge was busy. An arctic blizzard was a more appropriate name for the storm. With guilt, she had to admit that she was more concerned about Percy not appearing than Dana.

"They're here!" Mindy shouted, bouncing into the kitchen, ecstatic.

"Dana with them?" Lara asked, her throat dry. She'd forgotten to put on makeup!

Mindy scowled. "Of course not."

Lara took off her apron, having to make a conscious effort to keep her hands from trembling. Celeste gave her a thumbs-up.

"I'll finish up here and join you in a minute," she said. "Good luck."

"Take that gum out of your mouth," Lara said, following Mindy to the living room. "Makes you sound like a cow."

"How gross," Mindy said, swallowing it.

Cal was standing with his fingers hooked — macho style — in his pockets, talking to Nell. Percy was sitting on the bricks next to the fire, his gray sweat shirt rolled up, revealing dark muscular arms. Rachael, dazzling in tight, white dress pants and a black turtleneck sweater minus the bra, sat by his side, laughing gratefully at whatever he was saying, letting her fingers do all the things Lara had feared. Well, not *everything*. One thing you had to grant Rachael, she didn't waste any time.

"Hello," Lara said softly. There was a pause, eyes turning, Rachael's toward a window. Percy stood smoothly — every move he made had class — and squeezed the tops of her arms. Not an embrace, but it would do.

"Hi, Lara, so we made it after all," he said, smiling warmly, with a trace of amusement.

"Did you have trouble with the storm?"

"Not enough to keep us from coming."

Not enough to keep me away from you, Lara thought. This was not a crush. It was an obsession.

"Probably have to stay the night, though," Cal laughed, too loud.

"That wouldn't be a good idea," Nell said flatly.

"I smell food," Percy said, smoothing over the awkward moment. "Good food. Glad we didn't have the bite in the coffee shop."

Rachael rolled her tongue inside her mouth, not missing the reference to their having met a second time. Lara was pleased. "Celeste," she said, "she's our other friend, has been cooking us a feast. Oh, here she is now."

Like a timid deer, Celeste slipped into the room. Percy and Cal said hello. Celeste only nodded and smiled, remaining silent. Lara did not like the way Cal's eyes looked her over. There were really no two ways about it; he was a jerk.

"Looks like we're outnumbered," Cal told Percy with a snort.

"Where's Dana?" Percy asked.

"We're not sure," Lara said. "You haven't seen her?"

"No," Percy said. Cal shook his head.

"She'll show up," Rachael said, shifting the burning logs with the poker. "Nell, can we eat in here? So much more cozy than the dining room. I like fires."

"I don't care where we eat," Nell answered curtly, perhaps annoyed by the reference to fire.

Celeste and Nell took the job of servers. Back and forth they traveled to the kitchen, yet Lara received the distinct impression that they were timing their trips so as to avoid each other.

Dinner was a masterpiece. Chickens basted in rosemary, baked potatoes sliced through the middle and tucked with sour cream and butter, two casseroles of assorted vegetables coated with an inch of melted Swiss cheese, wild rice with minced green peppers and hot spices, two bottles of expensive red wine, and, of course, the artful carrot cake. They ate in a circle, Lara on Percy's right, and Rachael — ridiculously close — on his left. Nervous, Lara had no appetite, but nevertheless filled her plate. She had read in *Cosmopolitan* that men found women with huge appetites sexy.

Shamelessly, Mindy drooled over Cal, who fairly well ignored her, focusing his attention on Celeste, who couldn't have had a thing in common with him. Percy divided his attention between Rachael and Lara and, like in the coffee shop, mainly played the role of a good listener. Still, he sensed Nell's withdrawal and went out of the way to bring her into the flow of the conversation — successfully, too, with Nell relating for the first time how the house had originally belonged to a Vegas mafioso who had used it to store huge quantities of cocaine and heroin, up until his mysterious disappearance. In a subsequent probe, the FBI had found faint traces of human bones — this is what made the story interesting — in this very fireplace. Perhaps because of the wine, Nell went into greater detail than Lara cared for. Nell still hadn't bothered covering her scars with makeup.

"Reminds me of when I was in Germany," Cal said, emptying the second wine bottle into his glass. He had drunk more than all of them put together. Lara worried about the bottle of Bacardi 151 rum that he'd brought. That stuff was like kerosene.

"You were in Germany!" Mindy said, with such enthusiasm that it made even Celeste wince.

Cal broke off a corner of the half-eaten

cake and stuffed it into his mouth. "Was there two years," he chewed. "Love that German beer, those German women; man, they made a boy feel at home." He belched. "Anyway, what you said about that guy getting fried reminds me of this time we accidently napalmed these four Kraut soldiers. Hell, those Krauts thought Hitler was still on the throne, I swear. Couldn't stand those bastards."

"You burned four men to death?" Lara asked, her dinner moving in her stomach, her question angering Cal.

"*Accidently*, dear. We were on a copter hop, not far from the wall, when we lost our back blade. Started spinning like a damn top. Dumped the napalm we were carrying 'cause we thought we were going down. Man, we were in the middle of nowhere! No way I did it on purpose! I told that son of a bitch colonel that it had been an accident. He wouldn't listen to me." Cal chuckled. "Took them a month to identify those Krauts. You should have seen those flames. Better than Fourth of July." He finished his wine. "Made me feel proud to be an American."

Percy was following Cal closely. Apparently he had not heard the story before. Lara understood now why Cal had been discharged. She doubted that it had been an honorable one. Whoever heard of dumping napalm? Cal felt her disgust and looked at the floor, not happy with what he'd revealed. "I thought this was supposed to be a party," he said. "Where's the music?"

"We should play some games," Rachael said.

"I'm game," Percy said.

"Are you?" Rachael asked slyly, poking his side. "Know strip poker?"

Shyness was not one of Rachael's faults. And Percy was doing nothing to discourage her attention. "We could play charades," Celeste said, coming to life.

"Now, just what is that, young lady?" Cal asked.

"Where you tell someone a word or a phrase without saying it," Celeste said. "You use your hands, gestures."

"Can you write it down?" Cal asked, trying to concentrate.

"If you know how to write," Percy said. "Charades sounds good with me."

"Could you start without me?" Lara said, getting up. "I have to make a call."

"There's seven of us," Rachael said. "We can't have even teams."

"I want to be on Lara's side," Percy said.

The thrill of joy that pulsed through her veins almost forced her to sit down. "So do I," Celeste said.

"My, aren't we popular," Rachael said.

"I'll be on your team," Nell said to Rachael. "And we'll take Mindy and Cal."

Déja vu interrupted Lara's bliss — maybe

even a memory. *Why now?* She had played charades many times since *then.* "Be back in a sec," she said, going upstairs to the master bedroom, feeling as if she was running away. The number to the lodge was still fresh in her mind.

"Park Administration."

"Is this Roger McCormick?"

"Yes."

"This is Lara Johnson. I called earlier regarding Dana Miller?"

"I remember the voice. I'm sorry, Lara, she hasn't checked in here. You haven't heard from her?"

"No."

"I don't wish to sound like we are not concerned about the welfare of your friend, but to implement a full-scale search for her in this weather would be a major undertaking. Is there any reason whatsoever that she may be avoiding returning to your place?"

"Sort of. We're having a party and there's a guy here that she had a run-in with earlier."

"And she knew this young man was coming to your party?"

"Yes. But I still think she would have at least called. Maybe she's checked into the lodge?"

"Not under Dana Miller. I went over the names of all the visitors. You probably know that we have buses leaving here every hour before eight. Maybe she just went home. Where are you girls from?"

"Oakland."

"Have you called her family?"

"I hadn't thought of that. I'll do so."

"If you get a negative response, then it's up to you. You know your friend and the circumstances better than us. If you say so, then we'll start a search."

"Not yet," Lara said. Probably Dana had hated being mauled by Cal. And she'd had plenty of money to stay elsewhere or take a bus home. "Could I call you back in an hour or two?"

"I will be here all night."

"Thanks. Oh, did you check on the colonel?"

"I haven't had an opportunity to ask the boss about him. There is definitely no one on the roster by that name."

"I'm sure it's a nickname."

"I realize that. I don't have a definite answer for you."

Lara did not want to give her head too much to worry about. "Look, I'll call you later, Roger."

"Fine."

Dana's parents didn't answer. After twenty rings, Lara remembered that they, too, had been going away for the weekend.

She had only hung up the phone, and was preparing to join the others downstairs, when it rang. *Must be for Nell*, she thought.

calling on this line. To her surprise, it was Celeste's aunt.

"Lara, dear, how is your trip so far?"

"Fine." No sense bringing up Dana until she knew something more definite. "Would you like me to get Celeste? She's downstairs."

"Don't bother the girl. She'd probably be embarrassed to know that I've called. But I was sitting here alone and . . . the house seems so empty without her. How is she doing?"

"Real good. Didn't you talk to her earlier?"

"No."

"Are you sure?"

"I haven't spoken to her today, dear."

Why had Celeste lied? Lara thought back to their conversation: *"That wouldn't change. . . . I did."*

Celeste had wanted to say something else. Maybe she wasn't simply homesick.

"We're all having a good time," Lara continued. "Celeste made us an incredible meal. We were just about to play some games. You should see this house! I don't think any of us realized just how rich Nell's parents are."

"How is Nell?"

"Nell's okay. Do you know her, Mrs. Winston?"

"No — I mean, in a way, from listening to you girls talk about her. Listen, I'm going to let you get back to your friends. Don't even tell Celeste that I called. She had asked me not to."

"I understand," Lara said, not altogether sure that she did. Celeste's aunt was in an awful hurry to get off the phone. They exchanged take-cares and good-byes. Rachael was standing in the doorway.

"Who was that?" she asked.

"Celeste's aunt."

"What did she want?"

"To see that we were alive and well. She didn't want Celeste to know that she'd called."

Rachael plopped herself down in the corner in a chair. A gust of snow-laden wind shook the bedroom window. Outside was a black void. "Sometimes I wonder about that Celeste."

"What do you *wonder*?"

"Don't get hostile. Just something about her spooks me."

"She's twice the person either of us is."

"She's a sweet girl. But you've known her since the second day of school, and you don't know a damn thing about her."

"I've known you since I was four and I still haven't figured you out," Lara said deliberately, searching for a clue.

Rachael took the remark as a compliment. "Percy likes you," she said, baiting her own trap. Yet sitting face to face with Rachael, as she had done so many times through the years, Lara found it hard to believe that her motives were dangerously dark. She almost asked, who had been the guy on the other end of the line, what they had been talking about. Almost.

"What are we going to do?" Lara asked, taking an indirect stab at openness. "We have the whole night in front of us."

Rachael was cool. "The later it gets, the better I get. So he wants you on his team. I'm not putting up the white flag, Lara."

"You're the one who said it wasn't a war."

"I've changed my mind."

Lara stared her straight in the eye. "This one you're going to lose."

Rachael didn't flinch. "This battle maybe. But never the war, Lara."

Lara looked away, sighing. "At least we know where we stand. Before we return to the battlefield, there are a couple of things we must discuss. First, Dana. And don't tell me she'll show up soon."

Rachael was quiet for a moment. "All right, let's take a negative point of view. What *could* have happened to her?"

"She could have left the path to take a shortcut back to the lodge and broken a leg."

"But you didn't see any tracks leading off the path. I didn't."

"Except where we found that ski, I wasn't looking for them."

"Still, you would have noticed. And Nell's

right about that ski; it could have belonged to anybody. Probably someone just tossed it."

"Then what about their tracks? On one ski, they would have stood out like a sore thumb."

"Maybe they — whoever they are — broke a leg, and had a partner, and this partner carried them back to the lodge on their back, and managed to stay inside our grooves. I'm not Mrs. Holmes, but I suspect that Dana *never* left the path, but continued on, past the house, and wrapped around back to the lodge."

"Nell would have seen her."

"Not necessarily."

"But Nell was on the porch."

"Was Nell on the porch the whole time?"

"Did she say she wasn't?"

"Not exactly."

The answer disturbed Lara. Rachael was trying to be logical — always the approach of the villain — and that logic wasn't right. Perhaps reading her mind, Rachael added, "We have the perfect motive for her disappearing in her wanting to avoid Cal. You're making a mountain out of a . . . out of a snowball."

Lara was going to mention the two similar circular impressions in the ice but knew that it would lead to — from her side — supernatural hypothesis, which Rachael would have no tolerance for.

"We might have another problem," Lara said instead. "That character who took our car keys — the colonel — he's probably not a ranger." Briefly, she reviewed her conversations with Roger McCormick. And once again, Rachael tried to play down the situation.

"If he was a car thief, there's no way he would have hung around the lodge where he could be spotted. So Mr. McCormick didn't know him by the 'colonel'? You said yourself that probably isn't his real name."

"Aren't you worried about your car at all?"

"That's why my daddy pays for insurance, so I don't have to worry."

No problem with the car, Lara remembered. *To hell with her; she's just another fly to swat.*

"I see, Lara said softly. "And I suppose you're not worried about the melted snowman, either?"

"Huh?"

"Never mind."

"Oh, that! I haven't given it a second thought. What's gotten into you? You'd think you were on a paranoid acid trip. Let's get back to the boys. What are we going to do after charades? You should be worrying about that."

"Play with a Ouija board," Lara muttered, her nightmare nudging back in.

"With Nell here? Really, Lara, that would be gross."

"Sorry. You never think about it, do you?"

"What's the point?"

"Rach, I *want* you to think about it. Remember back to when you asked who the evil spirit was. You frowned, like something was wrong. Why did you frown?"

"Because it spelled Nicole's name!"

"No, it was something else. You had another reason."

"Isn't this a little off the wall?"

"Please, try to remember."

Rachael went to snap a quick retort, when suddenly she stopped, her eyes slipping far away. "There was a reason," she whispered.

"What?"

"The planchette, it . . . I can't remember. It was nothing important."

"Try harder."

"We were kids! I can't remember. To hell with it; it's past. Let's go play charades."

Celeste and Percy had already printed words on cards to use against the others: ecclesiastical, Lyndon Baines Johnson, rhubarb, Zimbabwe. Lara figured they had the game in the bag until she accidentally overheard one of the words Rachael was suggesting: the Rosicrucian Fellowship Ephermis 1950–1959. An uproar followed. All finally agreed to stick with current phrases.

Mindy went first. Lara gave her *Return of*

the Jedi to communicate. Nell held the stop-watch, and Mindy was onstage only forty seconds — it was too easy even for bubble-gum brain. Celeste went next and drew *Romeo and Juliet.* ("Is that current, Rach?" Lara had asked.) A master of body language, Percy was able to pick up Celeste's meaning inside twenty seconds. Lara was given *milk*, and suspected that Rachael was trying to embarrass her by subtly prodding her to squeeze her breasts, which she refused to do. Still, they all had fun, except for perhaps Cal, who was working on his Bacardi 151 and smelling totally wasted. Before his turn was up, Nell had to rewind the watch.

After an hour of play, Lara's team was destroying Nell's. Rachael demanded a shakeup. She wanted Celeste. So Rachael — Lara had to doubt her motives, because the move was totally illogical — and Celeste switched sides. Then something remarkable began to occur. No matter what word they gave Nell, Celeste guessed it almost immediately, and vice versa. Lara swore to herself that one of them must have telepathy. Cal continued to ruin their score, however. He also continued to eye Celeste, trying to charm her, actually touching her arm, her leg. She put him off politely. It was apparent that he made her nervous. Somehow Mindy had con-vinced herself that she didn't notice. Lara was searching for a tactful way to tell Cal to bug off, when he pinched Celeste's side.

She gave out a cry of genuine pain.

Nell leaped to her feet, exploding. "You fat slob! Who the hell do you think you are?! Get out of my house!"

"Nell," Celeste began weakly.

"Huh?" Cal slurred, not yet caught up with the present.

"Just get the hell out of my sight!" Nell swore.

"Lay off him!" Mindy, shouted, standing. "You're always bossing people around!"

"What?!" Nell said, stupefied. "What!?"

"He didn't do anything wrong!" Mindy yelled.

Nell sucked in a breath, like a dragon. "Here this jerk's supposed to be with you and he's hustling Celeste and *you're* defending him!?"

"You just hate everyone!" Mindy said stupidly. *Poor Mindy*, Lara thought. Nell was probably doing her a favor, though Nell was much angrier than made sense.

"Why don't we just—" Lara tried.

"No one calls me a jerk," Cal said angrily, stumbling to his feet.

"Oh, really, jerk?!" Nell snickered.

"Shut up!" Mindy shouted.

"Tight-face bitch," Cal said.

Percy finally decided to step in. He was too late. Even as he moved to prevent blows from falling, Nell kicked Cal's left shin with her hard-tipped leather boots. Cal's howl as he doubled up in pain promised a cruel vengeance. Still, even in his agony, he did not drop his glass of rum. Nell plucked it deftly from his hand to — so Lara assumed — throw it in his face. But the fumes of the drink reaching her nose — better than three-quarters alcohol — seemed to give her a new idea. Only cursing Cal separated her from raging Mindy, who stood with her back to the fire. Deliberately, with the beginning of a laugh, Nell threw the rum at her, the fiery liquid drenching Mindy's left arm.

"Nooo!!" Celeste cried in terror.

"My new blouse!" Mindy whined.

"For Christ's sake, it's my blouse," Rachael said, sounding incredibly bored.

Cal snorted at Nell like a charging bull. "You're going to pay for that, lady."

"Enough!" Percy said, positioning himself in front of Nell. Cal heaved forward anyway, his coordination a disaster. Percy grabbed him easily by the chest. When Cal struggled and spat in his face, Percy's eyes darkened and he drew back his fist and went for his roommate's jaw. Cal fell back like a dropped sack of potatoes. Mindy, of course, tried to catch him. Cal had to weigh a good two hundred pounds. Mindy fell backward also, close to the fire.

Too close to the fire.

Lara did not immediately realize that anything was seriously wrong. Her first thought was cynical: *That's one way to ruin a party.* Then she noticed Mindy's drenched arm draped over the bricks; Mindy staring at her arm, puzzled at something going on there. Above her, the air quivered like a desert mirage. Lara remembered in chemistry class how a dish of alcohol had burned with an invisible flame. And here and now, there wasn't Nicole's polyester robe and woolen sweater to fire it. Not unless the fire spread.

"Roll on the floor!" Rachael shouted, the words echoing from the past.

Mindy began to scream. Celeste flew from the room. Percy whipped off his sweat shirt and tried to smother Mindy's arm. But Mindy launched into a dancing frenzy and he couldn't catch her. Spontaneously Lara reached for the bottle — *because it was wet* — of liquor next to the sprawled Cal. Her eyes met Nell's, who was following her rather than Mindy. Nell shook her head faintly. Lara dropped the bottle.

"Hold her, damn it!" Rachael said. From God knows where she had a fire extinguisher in her hands. Percy dove, tackling Mindy at the knees. Rachael let loose a well-aimed jet of fog. A white coat blanketed the burning arm and one side of Percy's face. The fire was gone, with Mindy's breath coming in hysterical gasps. Lifting her up, Percy laid her gently on the couch. After a quick survey of the injury, he ripped back the blackened sleeve. Lara closed her eyes, imagining ashen bone, oozing dirty blood.

"Shhh," Percy said. "It's not bad. Mindy!

Listen to me! Your arm's fine. Little worse than a bad sunburn. Shh. . . . You're going to be okay. That's it. You're going to be just fine."

Mindy's spastic breathing subsided. She began to cry quietly. Lara dared a look. Percy was rubbing her forehead, speaking reassuring words. Lara knew that shock was the first danger to confront, and he was handling her perfectly. Lara wondered if she wasn't in shock herself. Already blisters were swelling on Mindy's red arm. There would follow incredible pain, probably scarring, yet compared to Nicole, this had been but a —

Warning, Lara.

What was that? Lara thought that Celeste had whispered in her ear. But when she looked, Celeste was gone. Cal was going, too. Nell had picked the poker from the fire — glowing cherry red at the end — and was pointing it at him.

"Do I make myself clear?" she said coldly.

Cal sobered quickly. "Wasn't my fault."

Nell shoved the rod two inches from his nose. Perspiration stood out on his forehead. "Get the hell out of here!" Nell said.

Cal searched for support, finding none. "Should have been you, bitch," he muttered, backing off and leaving. They heard the coat closet opening, the front door slamming. Lara sat on the couch beside Percy, taking Mindy's good hand.

"Do that dance at the prom," Lara said, "and you'll win the Richard Pryor Award."

"Michael Jackson's a better dancer," Mindy said, not getting the joke. Her back ached. "Ohhh! It hurts!"

"That's a good sign," Percy said, wiping the white powder from his face. "Shows that the burn didn't go so deep to where the nerves were destroyed. Everyone will think you just fell asleep under the sun lamp. I know you girls will do anything for a tan, even light yourselves on fire." This made Mindy smile. "Hey, Rachael, why don't you sit here for a minute with your wounded friend."

"Sure." Rachael did not appear the least flustered. Percy ushered Lara into the kitchen. "I feel responsible for this," he said. "I only wish I'd taken that drunk's head off when I hit him. But I must have been out of my mind to hit him with Mindy at his back and the fire right there."

He was more upset than he had allowed in the living room. "If it hadn't been for you —" Lara started to say.

"Cal wouldn't have banged into Mindy," he interrupted. "And Mindy's arm wouldn't have gone into the fire."

"But her arm didn't go into the fire."

"It went close enough." He sighed. "Call the lodge. See if we can get a doctor up here."

Roger McCormick was still at work. "Has Dana Miller showed up?" he asked. Lara ex-

plained their more pressing emergency. He
told her to hold the line, and was gone ten
minutes. When he returned, he said that he
was putting on a Dr. Kaminski.

"Can I help you?" a gentleman with a
Brooklyn accent asked.

"Our friend has burned her arm," Lara
said. "Can you come up? We're at Cedar
Springs, the Kutroff residence."

"How bad is it?"

"She's in a lot of pain."

Doctor Kaminski exchanged muffled words
with Roger McCormick, learning the distance that he would have to travel and how
miserable the storm was. Lara thought that
she heard him groan. "Tell me in detail how
it happened," he said finally, "what the injury looks like now, her mental state." Lara
described the "accidental" drenching with
the rum, the mass of sprouting blisters
across the entire inside of Mindy's arm.
Mindy's mental state was more difficult to
convey — usually she didn't seem to have
one — but Lara thought she got the situation
across. "Sounds like only second degree," the
doctor muttered. "I take it you've removed
the clothing over the wound?"

"Yes. Was that the right thing to do?"
Lara asked. Nell entered the kitchen.

"How is she?" Percy asked.

"Sore," Nell said.

"Elevate her legs slightly," Dr. Kaminski

said. "Also the injured arm. Do you have a first-aid kit, sterile gauze?"

Lara asked Nell, who nodded. "Yes, we do," Lara said. "But isn't there any way that you could come?"

"Everything I can do at this point, you can do also. Wrap her arm snugly in gauze. Keep her warm. At fifteen-minute intervals, give her a solution of half a teaspoonful of salt and half a teaspoonful of sodium bicarbonate to drink."

"What's that?"

"Baking soda. Your main job is to make sure she doesn't go into shock. From what you've described, that does not appear to be a danger. Nevertheless, keep her warm and keep an eye on her. Have her drink fruit juice if it doesn't make her nauseous."

"I have codeine," Nell said, handing Lara a prescription container. "Ask about these."

"Can we give her these pills for pain?" Lara asked. She read every letter and numeral on the label.

"If after an hour," Dr. Kaminski said, "she is still alert and shows no signs of metabolic depression, you may give her two, followed with plenty of liquids. But not for an hour. Call me immediately if there is a change in her condition. Call tomorrow in either case."

After thanking him, Lara hung up the phone and relayed the instructions.

"Leave her to me," Nell said. "I've had

lots of experience with bandages."

Lara was sure she had. "How is Celeste?" she asked.

"She's in her room," Nell said. "I would leave her alone for the time being."

"Sure upset her," Percy said.

"It would upset anybody," Nell said bitterly, leaving.

Lara's own reaction had taken longer, but now it hit with a force that humiliated her, forcing her to sit down, bringing a gush of tears. Percy sat beside her and did the very best thing, which was simply wait. Lara fought for control, finally managing an apology and explained, "It's just that it was so much like last time, like when Nicole died. How can it be a coincidence?"

"Who was Nicole?" Percy asked gently.

Even Lara did not realize the key to that question could be to Pandora's box. The story poured out, starting when she poured the liquor on Nicole, reversing in time to explain the circumstances, occasionally jumping to the present: the fried snowman, Rachael's sinister telephone conversation, the mysterious colonel, Cal's suspicious past, the inexplicable single ski, and Dana's disappearance.

She must have been making an incoherent conspiracy out of everyone and everything, for Percy finally interrupted, saying, "The only *real* question is, Where's Dana? The rest almost certainly has nothing to do with that question."

Lara was momentarily crushed. She had been hoping for support. "What about the things Rachael said?"

Percy glanced to the kitchen entrance, careful not to be overheard. Snowflakes bombarded the blocked window above the table like mute machine-gun fire. Cold radiated through the wall at her back. Percy spoke in a low voice. "How often in the course of conversation have you said — innocently, without thinking — 'I wish I could kill her,' or, 'If only we could get rid of him'? Rachael strikes me as a very attractive, shrewd young lady. But not as someone capable of murder."

Why did he have to mention how attractive she was? "You don't know her like I do." Just sour grapes.

"A conspiracy between Cal and Rachael is out of the question. They scarcely spoke to each other when we all met at the mall."

"You mainly talked to her, right?"

"Right."

"Was Cal on the phone around seven?" she asked defensively.

"I was taking a nap. I'm not sure."

"So he could have been?"

"Lara."

"I know, I know," she muttered in apology, pressing her hands against her eyes. "You see, I'm not saying what I really mean." Because she did not know. How could one explain a feeling, a haunting intuition, even to one's own self?

"I understand. You're upset over Mindy, worried about Dana."

"I'm worried about the snowman, too!" she burst out. His eyes were sympathetic, and *that* was no way to start a relationship. "All right, all right, so *all* these events are not connected. There is a pattern in *some* of them."

"What?"

"Fire!"

"Lara."

"Listen to me!" God, she sounded like her mother. "That snowman was in the shade. How could he melt by himself? And when we found Dana's ski, it was like the area had suddenly been blasted by heat, and left to freeze over. And when Mindy got burned just now, her arm didn't go in the fire."

"It didn't have to. The fumes ——"

"And when Nicole exploded," Lara went on, not listening, "I could have sworn to the Pope that I'd poured wine on her and not brandy. Wine couldn't have done that to her."

"What does a nine-year-old know about different types of alcohol? Nothing! You yourself mentioned the guilt you suffered after the accident. Well, it is simply surfacing again."

"No!" Lara pounded the table, disturbing the salt and pepper shakers. "There is *something* behind this!"

"What?"

"I told you. Fire! It's coming from somewhere." She quieted. "Or from *someone*. Percy, have you ever read about pyrokinetics, SHC?"

"Spontaneous human combustion? In the *National Enquirer*, alongside articles on people who've been taken aboard alien space craft from the Andromeda galaxy and had their tonsils removed."

"You don't believe in things like that?"

"I'm skeptical, very skeptical. Are you saying that Dana suddenly decided to cook herself?"

"No. I'm suggesting that maybe — just as a possibility — someone burned her. With their mind."

"Like in that movie *Carrie?*"

"Sort of."

"That was a movie, Lara. Mindy had an arm drenched in alcohol next to a blazing fire before she lit up."

Lara took a couple of deep breaths. "I know what you're saying is the logical point of view. I spoke to Nell and Rachael, and they were logical, too. But I can't get rid of this feeling. It keeps coming back."

"What are we going to do about it?"

"Stop sitting around and waiting for Dana to show up, for one thing. Where I found her ski on the path, I made a cross out of branches and fastened it to a tree. I can find that place again. Can I — would you mind if

I walked part of the way back with you?"

Percy smiled, the same gesture that seemed somehow different each time, richer and warmer as she came to know him better. She was still roller-coasting in the infatuation stage, but she had crested at a peak and could see a glimmer of light in the distance that said that maybe there was something real here. At least through her eyes. He was reading her mind. "I was hoping, Lara, that you were going to ask me to stay."

"Yeah? No. I mean — I would like you to stay. But, I . . . I don't know. I don't know anything at this point." She bowed her head, trying to untangle her thoughts. What the hell, bare her heart for everyone to see. "I like you," she whispered.

"I like you."

She glanced up. "Really? No you don't. Do you?"

"Of course."

"I don't believe you."

"You better. I've already made plans how I'm going to visit you in Oakland."

Lara felt giddy all of a sudden, yet still worried. "But you must know lots of girls. You probably like lots of them, like Rachael. I know how pretty she is."

"Rachael's very pretty."

"Oh, I know." Hard to walk this razor's edge, when she was sweating like this.

"But she's not you. I like you. What does Rachael have to do with that?"

Lara, to her total humiliation, began to cry again. "I'm sorry," she shook her head, wiping her face, looking anywhere but at him. "I'm usually not like this. I never cry. Never!"

"You've just had a rotten day." He took her hand.

She blushed. "Not all rotten. I met you."

"Still want to go to the spot?"

She nodded. "I won't sleep tonight unless I do."

"Very well. But let's stay that hour with Mindy the doctor recommended before starting down."

Nell and Rachael should have been RN's. Mindy was professionally bandaged, resting on the couch with her bad arm and two legs elevated with pillows, trying unsuccessfully to convince Rachael that there was no way she was going to go into shock and why the hell didn't they give her at least one of the codeine pills?

Lara excused herself after a few minutes — under Nell's watchful eye — and went to find Celeste. The door to her room was open, the light out. Celeste was lying face down on the bed.

"Celeste? It's Lara. Mindy's okay. Can I come in?"

"Is the doctor coming?" she asked sadly, not stirring.

Lara sat on the bed beside her. "No. Mindy's not that hurt."

"But she was on fire."

"Rachael put it out as quick as it started. Go talk to her yourself, and you'll see."

"I don't want to. I don't want to hurt her."

"Nonsense. You'll cheer her up."

"I don't want to hurt any of you."

"Look at me, Celeste. You're beginning to sound as crazy as me. Come, let's go downstairs."

"No."

"Why not?"

"It was my fault."

"You didn't have anything to do with —" Lara stopped.

Someone burned her. With their mind.

Celeste sensed her sudden fear, rolled over, and stared at her. Celeste had extraordinary eyes, a cat's hypnotic emerald gaze, glittering with faint light from the hall. "Don't you know?" she asked from a place far away. "I think you know."

Lara stood, backing off. "Know what?"

"Why Mindy got burned." Celeste closed her long-lashed eyes — a mild tremor shaking her body — opened them again slowly, the gesture curiously reptilian. "I think you remember."

Lara was having difficulty breathing. The air was *hot*. "Remember what? Nell splashed her with alcohol and Mindy fell next to the fireplace. . . . *Why was it your fault?*"

Celeste put a pillow over her face. "Everything I've told you is a lie," she said, her voice thick. "I won't lie to you anymore. Just get out of this place while you still can."

"I don't understand."

Celeste did not answer. Her breathing said that she had gone to sleep. Lara would have shaken her and questioned her further, but she didn't want to. She was afraid to touch her.

Downstairs, Nell asked how Celeste was. "Asleep," Lara answered.

At the end of the hour, Percy gave Mindy two pills with a glass of orange juice and carried her upstairs to her bedroom. She was asleep before they could tuck in the sheets. Awfully strong medicine. Nell left the pills atop her nightstand and the light on in case "she awoke in the night in pain."

Rachael suggested coffee, and Percy thought that sounded good. With the four of them sitting at the kitchen table, Rachael said, "You're staying, aren't you, Percy?"

"I don't think so."

Rachael smiled and refilled his cup. "Sure you are. With the two of us already out of action, you should be able to protect yourself."

"My parents wouldn't want any boys staying overnight," Nell said.

"Your parents aren't here," Rachael said.

Nell ignored her, and spoke to Percy. "Myself, I'd like you to stay. But I'm sure you understand."

"No problem."

Rachael simmered, threatening to boil. If Nell and Rachael had an all-out clash, the house would melt. It was ironic, too, since in so many ways they were similar. "Why should he have to ski four miles through this kind of weather?" Rachael asked.

The grandfather clock in the living room struck an ominous midnight. *Time to take off our masks*, Lara thought, *and show who was behind Rachael's sensual lips, Celeste's haunting eyes, Nell's plastic features.* Lara stared at her own face, which reflected like a lifeless shadow in the icy, black window. That's how she would look when she was dead.

"I don't make the rules," Nell said firmly.

"You just love enforcing them," Rachael muttered sarcastically. Lara knew her plan. Wait till they were all asleep and then tiptoe stark naked to where Percy was sleeping and ask him to scratch an itch that she couldn't quite reach. Lara trusted Percy's loyalty. Nevertheless, she also wanted him out of the house. No reason to test him. None at all.

"Shut up, Rachael," Nell said dryly.

Blood burned Rachael's cheeks. "I will pretend that I did not hear that."

Nell sipped her coffee. "Then I will have to say it again."

"You two stop it!" Lara said. "Don't you know we have a guest?"

"Sorry, Percy," Nell said.

"I'm sorry, too," Rachael grumbled.

Percy finished his cup with a single gulp and got to his feet. "Nothing worse than a guest who has overstayed his welcome. I'm the one who should be apologizing. When I see Cal, I'll be sure to hit him again. I'm going to get my skis, Lara."

She nodded. "We better get started."

"We? We?" Rachael said, wrinkling her forehead.

"Lara wants to recheck the spot where she found Dana's ski," Percy said. "She's going to follow me part way back."

"I was going to recommend that," Nell said. "It's a good idea."

"And walk back alone in this storm?" Rachael said. "It's a stupid idea."

"I'll be just fine," Lara said.

"You know," Percy said, thinking, "maybe someone should be there to walk back with you." Lara shook her head minutely.

"I'll come," Rachael said.

"Don't," Lara said.

"Why not?" Rachael asked.

All tact had gone out the window earlier in the evening. "Because I don't want you to," Lara said.

"Hurry back," Nell said, chuckling.

Rachael held her wrath in check. "Hope I see you again soon, Percy," she said, getting out of her chair and giving him a blatent hug and kiss, nuzzling his chest briefly with her body, leaving the guy with something to think about. Percy, to Lara's immense satisfaction, did not return the kiss.

"I'm sure we will," he said.

"Can I help you with your skis?" Rachael asked.

"No," he said. "Why don't you two just stay here and relax and finish this pot of coffee."

Rachael took the hint and remained in the kitchen with Nell. Lara knew that they would do anything but relax together. In the short hallway at the main entrance to the house, she had finished lacing up her boots, when she remembered her scarf in the living room. "I've got to get something," she told Percy.

Resting neatly folded on the bricks by the fireplace, inches from where Mindy had caught fire, she found Rachael's scarf, the one the snowman had been wearing. Since her own mother had knitted the scarf, Lara decided to wear it instead.

She heard angry voices coming from the kitchen.

"Cal, my foot!" Rachael was saying. "You're the one who threw the alcohol on Mindy!"

"No, I was trying to hit him!"

"You missed by a solid six feet!"

"Are you saying that I did it on purpose!?"

Lara hurried away before she had to hear anymore. She knew they were just warming up.

Chapter 6

The outside thermometer read minus-ten degrees. Fortunately the wind had abated considerably, although Percy maintained that the storm was merely catching its breath. Both of them wore nifty flashlights that hung around their necks, clearly illuminating the width of the path and the unrelenting falling snowflakes. Beyond their circle of light, the frozen landscape was a *Twilight Zone* background prop. The silence was pervasive, unnerving.

Lara spoke mainly to hear the sound of her voice. "Did Cal have a light?"

"Yes," Percy called over his shoulder, picking up speed. "You're wearing it."

"Why didn't he take it?"

"He was drunk. And Nell was about to brand him."

"How could he find his way back in the dark?"

"Good question. Don't worry about him."

She had to stop talking in order to match his pace, and to keep from running into him. Braking her momentum was more exhausting than maintaining it. She concentrated on his twin skis, imitating his moves. As a result, she almost missed the mysterious spot. Percy had crept thirty yards in front. His sudden descent and rise out of a dip clued her.

"Stop!" she called, sitting down, snow piling between her legs. Percy initiated an effortless one-eighty and helped her up. A cross hung on an adjacent tree.

"This it?" he asked.

"Pretty sure."

"What are we looking for, anyway?"

"Evidence." She went down on her knees, brushing snow away in armfuls. Her left knee, the one she had injured when Rachael had tried to kill her, began to lock up. It would be a weary road up the mountain.

"Look at this ice." She waved Percy to her side. "See how it curves down. If we brushed all this snow away, we would find a concave dish, like I did earlier. See how dirty the ice is?"

"Looks like dirt, plain dirt. Are you saying that it's ash?"

If she was, she was saying that they were standing on Dana's grave. "How many feet of snow was there prior to today's storm?"

"As much as seven or eight feet."

"Let's imagine a weird scenerio. Try to be open-minded. We will assume that SHC and pyro-kinetics exist. If Dana had been skiing along this path, and had suddenly caught fire, the best thing she could have done was roll in the snow. But from experience, I know people don't do the best thing. They try to run away from the fire. She would have jumped out of her skis, maybe out of only one of them, and run up the path. Now let's say our mysterious force really began to burn her. The articles I read said that some people were reduced to only a handful of ashes. Given that, she would have melt literally a ton of snow. A pool of water would have frozen. Naturally it would be lower than the surrounding snow. There would be left only scattered tracks leading nowhere. No body. The perfect crime. What do you think?"

"I think that you have a vivid imagination, but I don't suppose that's what you want to hear. Even from an occult point of view, you're standing on — forgive the pun — thin ice. You're conveniently mixing pyro-kinetics and spontaneous human combustion. They're separated phenomena."

"In my book, they're close enough."

"And you're talking about a power level that is way beyond anything that has even been dubiously demonstrated."

"If you accept the possibility, why does there have to be a limit to it?"

"You're beginning to sound like a para-psychologist. Okay, I'll grant you every possibility. Who's the source?"

And wasn't that the question of the hour. "I suspect everyone."

"Even me?"

She had to smile. "Except you."

Percy scared the hell out of her by suddenly catching fire! But no — God, her heart was going to burst — he had merely lit a flare.

"Don't ever do that!" she cried.

"Sorry." He saw how upset she was. "I thought all this speculating was getting us nowhere. I was going to melt some ice and study it. I should have warned you, I've always been one for theatrics."

She nodded, trying to calm herself. "I'm sorry I snapped at you. I never do that — God, I said that about crying. You must think I'm a real case."

"You're right. But you're a cute case."

"Really? No."

"Yes."

They were debating life and death, forces beyond the physical universe, and she forgot it all when he told her she was cute. "You're cute, too," she said.

He laughed. "Don't you think I know that?"

She moved closer, careful not to light herself on fire, feeling suddenly brave. "No laughs, I'm serious."

For all his class, his confidence, he seemed touched. He tossed the flare aside. "I'm going to kiss you." He put his hands on her shoulders and leaned forward. Lara closed her eyes, tilted her head back, and waited. And waited, feeling like Scarlett O'Hara. She ventured a look. Percy was worried.

"I'm not going to stop you," she said.

Poor boy, his conscience was getting in the way. "You're still in high school," he said nervously.

"Do I look like I'm in high school?"

"Not really."

"Then forget that I am. I'm eighteen!" Actually she was seventeen. "The law won't come after you."

"That's not what I was thinking! I just want you to know that I'm not the type of guy who tries to take advantage of the situation."

"Percy, it is ten degrees below zero. You're not going to take off my clothes, and I very much doubt that you want me to undress you. You *can't* take advantage of *this* situation."

He laughed. "This is a side of you that I haven't seen before."

Lara laughed, too. "I haven't seen it before either."

He kissed her. His nose was cold, his lips warm. She felt good in his arms, as if she wanted to stay there a long, long time. Hadn't a poet said that talk of death was the most potent aphrodisiac? She had never *done it* before, had always thought girls who did it on the spur of the moment without protection were fools. Yet she suddenly found herself wishing that it was a warm summer night with thick beds of grass behind the trees. He slipped his arms inside her coat at the back, picking her up slightly. His mouth tasted like carrot cake. She loved carrot cake. She leaned into him at the waist. He slipped and landed on his back. She went along for the ride, bursting into giggles.

"What happened?"

"The flare melted some snow," he said, slightly dazed. Men were such pushovers. "I slipped in the water."

"Are you okay?" She brushed snow off his ears.

"I'm just glad you didn't bite my tongue off."

"Could have done worse," she smiled, amazed at her own nastiness. Good old honorable Percy didn't get the joke. He rolled over onto his knees, killing the intimacy of the moment.

"Let's check your ice. The flare has melted a good chunk of it."

"That is what I came for," Lara muttered, disappointed.

Their diagnosis was uncertain. The snow had a dark substance in it, could have been ash, probably wasn't. Lara wanted to dig deeper. Percy was reluctant, mentioning the time, how far he still had to hike. "Now if I was staying at your place," he said, "we could dig up the entire path."

"I'd love to smuggle you in." She hugged

him from behind. In the morning she would not believe the things she had said and done. "But Nell would freak. Not to mention Rach."

"We'll be quiet."

"Ohh, I'm very loud," she said, on the threshold of hearing.

"What?"

"Nothing! And you were the one who was afraid to kiss me!"

He was indignant. "I wasn't afraid. I was just —"

"Being a gentleman. I know."

He drew from his coat pocket what looked like a swollen pistol. "Take this, it's a flare gun. It's loaded, and there's a refill. You just snap the flare in. You should always have one of these if you're hiking at night. Hold it out and away from your body, pointed at the sky, if you have to fire it."

"Looks dangerous," Lara said, stuffing it in her pants pocket.

"Just don't shoot anyone with it."

"Maybe Rachael."

"Hey, she's okay."

"Okay, huh?"

Percy hugged her tightly. "Don't worry, you're more than okay."

"Hey, I didn't give you my phone number."

"I'll probably see you before the weekend's up."

"You might not."

"Sure I will."

She broke free of his hold. Her stomach began to ache. Don't you want my phone number?"

"What for?"

"What?..." She was stumped. He laughed.

"I have it already."

"Who?"

"Oakland Information. I even got them to give me your address on Park View Lane."

She slugged him in the stomach. "Don't do that to me!"

"You look cute when your face falls."

"When did you call them?"

"I'm not going to tell you."

"Probably *immediately* after you met me in the coffee shop."

"Now listen to her!"

"Where does Rachael live?"

"I'm not going to tell you." She went to hit him again. "Okay. Okay. I don't know."

"You said the right thing, partner." She fixed his wool cap on his ears. A gust of wind had knocked it askew. The eye of the hurricane was passing. And so, it seemed, was the gaiety of the moment. Perhaps the cold was finally beginning to penetrate. Percy felt it, too.

"You're still limping. I'm going to ski back with you. Then I'll leave."

"You wouldn't leave. I wouldn't let you." Intuitively she knew Percy must not return to the house. Not because of Rachael, but because she really did care for him, and — *Just get out of this place, while you still can* — she wanted him to be safe.

Celeste had some explaining to do. All of them did.

"Go now, before I change my mind," she said, kissing him briefly on the lips. "Call me Monday if we miss each other."

"At six in the morning."

"I'll be up and waiting. Good-bye, Percy. Don't . . . forget me."

He turned and waved once as he skied away. Before she could respond, he rounded a bend and was gone. It would be a dark road for him. Maybe darker for her.

Haven't forgotten you, Dana. Laughter had disappeared with her best friend. Arguing and suspicion had dominated the night. Lara stepped to the center of the impression and dug the snow aside, using a sharp-tipped granite rock at the side of the path to crack into the speckled ice. The flare had gone out. She spent twenty minutes getting a foot deep, the gray thickening. A large chip, particularly dark, broke free. It would have to do. Her knee had gone passed tightening to cramping. Lara put the lump of ice in her pocket.

If the wind hadn't been at her back, she wouldn't have made it. By the time she sighted the house, her lungs were on fire and her leg was saying not another step. Except for a dull orange glow spilling through the living room windows, the house was dark.

She rested on the floor of the entrance hall for a spell before her hands thawed to where she could unlace her boots. No one came to welcome her home.

Nell was lying alone in the living room on the couch by the fire. Lara thought she was asleep, until she spoke, not opening her eyes.

"Did you find what you wanted, Lara?"

"I didn't find Dana." Lara sat across from her. The fire should have felt good, but it didn't. "Did the lodge call?"

"The phones are dead."

Lara's pulse quickened. "How?"

Nell didn't care. "The storm."

"Do you have a CB?"

"Somewhere."

"Where's Rach?"

"Asleep."

"Celeste?"

"Asleep, I suppose. Her door is locked."

"Why did she lock her door?"

"I guess she doesn't want to be disturbed."

"You and Rachael were really going at it when I left."

"We resolved our differences."

"That's good." Sparks burst from the logs. Lara's nerves were shot, and she jumped a foot out of the chair. Nell opened her eyes.

"Did you find anything?"

"No."

"Nothing?"

"Snow. Dirty ice."

"You've had a bad day, haven't you?"

"I met Percy. But otherwise, yeah, it's been rotten. I've been worrying all day, that's for sure."

"I had a lot of bad days," Nell said, shifting from laziness to anger.

"You mean, after the accident?"

"My whole life's been 'after the accident.' I don't remember anything before then. Do you?"

Lara took a chance. "I remember Nicole."

"Do you really? I don't think so. In fact, I know so."

Lara had no good response. "I'm sorry," she whispered.

"I knew you would recheck where you had found the ski," Nell said, as if that were related. She sat up, stabbed the fire with the poker. A flare illuminated her face, the shifting shadows emphasizing her scars. "You're looking at my scars," Nell said.

"You didn't wear makeup this weekend. Why?"

"What have I got to hide from any of you?" Nell chuckled. "Did Percy tell you how cute you were?"

"You still hate me, don't you?"

Nell dropped the poker, closed her eyes, held her breath for the longest time. "If it wasn't for —" she began, cutting herself off quickly. A single tear formed slowly, rolled down her cheek, divorced from the rest of her features, which remained as impassive as a mask. "The strangest thing is," she whispered, "I don't. I should, but I don't. Now I feel — I feel nothing." She shook herself, picked up the poker again, prodding the flames. "Go to sleep, Lara. It's late."

"You, too. You need to rest." Lara circled behind the couch, squeezed Nell's shoulders.

"In a bit I will rest."

"Are you worried about Dana?"

"I worry about all of you."

"A moment ago, you were going to say, 'If it wasn't for Nicole,' weren't you?"

"No, I wasn't. Not exactly. Good-night, Lara."

Lara dragged her feet slowly up the stairs. An exhaustion that penetrated her bones began to overwhelm her. In one day she'd walked more miles, suffered more nervous traumas than she ordinarily went through in a year. To close her eyes and forget everything, if only for a little while, was the answer to her most fervent prayer. But to reach her room she had to pass the others' rooms. Tired as she was, would she be able to sleep without questioning them?

Mindy's light was on. Not knocking, Lara tiptoed in. Mindy's loud snores didn't miss a beat. The top of the codeine pills was off. She reread the label. The container was supposed to hold forty tablets. There was no way that many pills that size would have fit. Lara hoped Mindy hadn't swallowed any more. Yet shock victims didn't snore and she left reassured after retucking Mindy's blankets.

Rachael's door was shut, the light out. Lara knocked, called softly. There was no answer. Rachael mustn't want to speak to her. Lara knew that she was an extremely light sleeper. She contemplated forcing the issue, but decided against it. She didn't have the strength left for a major confrontation.

At Celeste's door, she went through the same motions. No answer. She tried the handle. Locked.

"It's Lara, Celeste. Open up."

Fatigue prevented her from persevering. She pulled herself into her room, leaning on the door to shut it. The chunk of ice in her coat pocket banged her leg, calling for attention. But it was still frozen. She put it on the desk beneath the heating vent. In the morning the water would have evaporated and she could study at leisure what was left. In the dresser mirror she saw how red her eyes were. She pulled her pants half down, fell back onto the bed, her coat still on. In a minute she would go the bathroom and change into her pajamas and brush her teeth and turn off the light and get into bed properly. In just a second. . . .

Yet already she was sinking, gliding gently down a dark well with the promise of a wet bottom where all images of fire and ash would be washed clean. Rachael wouldn't kill her. Nell didn't hate her. Cal was far away. The colonel was a good guy. Dana was safe. Celeste wasn't a second Carrie. The snowman had gone peacefully. All was well.

Lara awoke with a jolt, an alarm screaming inside her skull. Before she could even figure her location, she fell off the bed and smashed nose first into the floor. It was a fire alarm, and this was it, they were all going to burn.

In reality her alarm clock was merely shouting that it was three A.M., twenty-four hours to the minute since she had gotten up to come on her wonderful weekend in the mountains. She had been unconscious exactly an hour. She flattened the ringing with her palm. A bottle of double-extra-strength aspirin wouldn't have dented her headache. Her mouth was as dry . . . as dry as the desk top! The ice had dematerialized, giving up its secrets. Lara scampered to her knees.

Ten seconds later found her vomiting in the toilet. There had been flakes of ash surrounding a single black piece that could only have been charred bone. All along, it had only been in her head. She could tell others of her worries and they could reason with her and then she would feel better. Dana was at the lodge. Dana was on the bus. Dana was at home. Sure, guys.

Dana was dead.

If I couldn't get into heaven, I wouldn't mind spending the rest of eternity here.

Part of Dana was on the desk. Which part?

Lara choked on dry heaves. She wanted desperately to pass out but she knew if she did she would never wake up. She had to get out of the house! Too many horror flicks had made it clear that if she stayed she would end up as dog meat. And — God forgive her — she had to leave alone. Mindy was drugged. Rachael had no scruples about swatting another fly. Nell couldn't forget. Celeste had no past. None of them could be trusted.

Lara stood slowly, pulling up her pants, ordering herself not to make a false move. Don't flush the toilet. Don't let anyone know you're awake. Zip up your jacket. Get your gloves. Put on your shoes. Turn out the light. So far, so good. She stepped quietly toward the door. Her knee buckled. Pain, Lara, as if it was actually on fire. She stifled a cry of despair. She would never get down the mountain on this leg. The CB? Even if there was one, she would have to ransack the house to find it. A pyro murderer wouldn't go for that. Had Cal really left? They'd all heard the door slam, but the house was big enough to hide him and his supply of napalm. The snowmobile in the basement! The keys were in the ignition! And Nell had said it was as easy as driving a car!

Lara crept into the black hall, wondering

if the pyro murderer had burned out the lights. Of course, they probably had a multitude of wicked weapons. She took a step forward. Maybe a cold steel knife in her spine, a stainless razor across the soft flesh of her throat. She steadied herself against the invisible wall. She knew she'd feel the blood spurting, warm and sticky; no one died immediately. She passed Celeste's room, Rachael's, Mindy's, all dark. Her parents would have to identify her body. The red glow coming from the living room reminded her of a descent into hell as she started down the stairs. There wouldn't be much left. Cut to pieces, then poured with gasoline. Or else fried by the hyperactive frontal lobes of a witch. The living room was filled with moving shadows, otherwise empty. No way she was going into the basement without a weapon. But the shotguns on the walnut mantle were unloaded. Is that all that's left of our daughter? her parents would wail. She approached the fireplace, the poker. There would be an article in the local paper, beneath her happy senior picture: was on the homecoming court, such a nice girl. Had her whole life in front of her. She weighed the poker in her hands. Swung hard it would split open someone's skull. Survived by Clara and James Johnson. Whoever she saw first was going to get it.

The door to the basement was ajar, casting a silver sliver of light onto the thick carpet. Lara peeked in, opening the door a millimeter at a time. A row of steps, three quick hops, and she could be behind the wheel with her hand on the key. Never mind the garage door, she would rev into first and waste whatever was in her way, all in only fifteen seconds.

But Lara took an eternity to open the door to where she could squeeze past. Even standing on the platform at the top of the steps, she did not have a clear view of the basement; hanging fiberglass insulation got in her way. She waited, trying not to breath or think, listening. Had she been breathing normally, she probably would have noticed the smell of kerosene immediately. When she did notice, she would have vomited again had she anything left in her knotted stomach.

Who are you, evil spirit in the basement?

An unseen plastic container contacted the basement's cement floor. A gurgle of kerosene followed; another container bounced. Lara did not remember dropping the poker, but she definitely heard when it hit the hot water tank. The noise must have echoed through the entire house. The pouring kerosene halted. She did not wait for the Who's there? She leaped back, slamming the basement door shut. Pursuing feet rushed up the steps. She threw the bolt. Fists pounded from the other side. She ran out the front door without her skis, down the powdery path in her thin canvas sneakers that sank two feet with each stride, on a knee made of foam rubber, not once glancing over her shoulder.

Her chances were lousy. The storm had regrouped into a thousand vicious tornadoes. The flakes stinging her eyes were more painful than blasted sand. Nothing in her experience had prepared her to even imagine a blizzard of this intensity. With no light, no strength, no Percy. She was almost doomed to die. But she would not go back. Death was not always the same. Freezing was infinitely preferable to burning.

She was stumbling blindly when her hands encountered a wall of ice. There must have been an avalanche of sorts; it had not been there a couple of hours ago. She tried to circle around, almost trapping herself in sharp bushes that lined the path. Swimming straight through was the only course. She was well on her way to the other side of the snow heap when her feet lost all support. *Down, Lara, you'll smother if you won't burn.* Quicksand, the wind-torn sky vanishing as snow covered her head. She screamed. Ice stuffed her throat. Sinking. Sinking. Only seventeen years old. It wasn't fair!

When she came to a standstill, she realized that if she stopped all her shouting, she could breathe quite easily. But what was the use? The lodge could just as well have been on the far side of the moon for all the hope she had of reaching it. And she was *so* tired. She closed her eyes, thinking to rest for a moment. Cold seeped through her coat. Not an uncomfortable cold that made her wish to be warm again. But a cold that whispered that if she just remained still a while longer, then she would never have to be cold again. There was no reason to fight the inevitable. A delicious warmth spread through her chest. How fine, not to even have to breathe anymore. *That's right, Lara. Rest and relax. Everything is all right. Soon you will be with Dana.*

"No!" she cried in horror, recognizing her folly. "No! Damn you, whoever you are, I will not die!"

Lara clawed at the ice in front of her. Terror was no longer her sole inspiration. Revenge gave her strength. Dana's murderer, even if it was the Devil himself, was going to pay. Snow shoved through her jacket collar. A razor edge of ice sliced her cheek. Blood spurted and froze. Suddenly the wall of ice tumbled, and she fell forward, the biting wind returning. She was through.

Yet anger brought her less than a mile farther. Her legs would no longer work, no matter how she bullied them. On hands and knees she gained at best an additional two hundred yards. Then she could no longer feel her hands and knees, or her arms, or her face, or even her blood pumping in her heart, only a pain inside that cried at all she would miss. Percy would call early Monday morning, and no one would be awake to answer. At graduation there would be a diploma with honors with her name on it, and she wouldn't be there to accept it. Her birthday would come, and her mother would have no reason to bake a cake. Her mother had always hated to bake, anyway.

"I will not die," she croaked, huddling into a ball. To revive her fingers to wipe the freezing tears out of her eyes, she pulled off her gloves with her teeth and shoved her hands into her crotch. She met an obstruction pressing through from her pocket.

The flare gun! She pulled it out and reached for the trigger, but it promptly slipped from her numb grasp and sank in the snow. Practically ripping her cheeks, she shoved her right hand in her mouth and licked her fingers frantically, getting a painful tingle. Next she banged her hands together so hard that she was sure she must be breaking bones. Still she could not master the delicate trigger. Inspiration gave her a third method of defrostation. She squeezed her hands back in her pants and — what the hell, she was going to die anyway — peed on them. That worked.

Like a firework from Mexico, the flare popped into the sky, a bulb of yellow light that detonated in a red brilliance that was nevertheless almost entirely swallowed by the low flying clouds. A ranger a mile away wouldn't even have seen it. Nice try, Percy. She reloaded the gun, but didn't even bother to fire the flare, shoving it in her belt under her coat. The brief crimson dawn faltered and died. The returning darkness was devastating.

I will not die, she thought, knowing that she would. Already her body was no longer attached to what was left of her mind. At least she didn't feel it. She hardly felt anything. Funny how she could still see. Her eyes must have frozen open. They would find her that way, staring forever down the path for help that never came. And this person surrounded by a bright light coming up the path to her rescue was surely a hallucination. Or perhaps it was tomorrow and she was already dead and simply hanging around to see herself found. Or maybe he was even an angel. The light was so bright, she wanted to blink, but couldn't. He moved closer. He was tall. He was overweight and had an unshaven face and baggy trousers and wasn't even that handsome. Some angel; you would think because she had been such a good girl and had gotten good grades and hadn't even had sex once that they would have sent a beautiful seraph.

"Lara," he said, staring down at her from an Olympian height of six feet. He was no angel. And she was not dead, though she suddenly wished that she were.

It was Cal.

She remembered nothing else.

Chapter 7

There were voices, warm light, thick air that smelled funny. The voices — they were rather annoying — were trying to wake her up. Lara wished they wouldn't bother. She'd had enough excitement for one day.

"Wake up, Lara."

"Leave me, Dana, I'm dead," she muttered.

"Wake up, you jerk."

That was Rachael, and how dare she call her a jerk. Lara opened her eyes. She was on the floor of the basement. "What's the deal?" she asked the sagging insulation and the hot water tank.

"I think she's awake," Dana said.

"Maybe it would have been better to leave her unconscious," Rachael said.

Lara went to sit up and couldn't. She was no longer numb but bound. She rolled on her side. Dana smiled at her.

"Dana! What relief! I thought you were dead."

"I wouldn't start celebrating just yet," Dana said. "You will note the fact that we are tied up in a basement filled with kerosene."

Dana lay to her left, wearing the same clothes as when Lara had last seen her, plus yards of clothesline string and spools of duct tape — as were they all — around her feet and hands. Rachael was flat on her back on the other side, her once shiny blond hair streaked with blood, her face ashen. At the far end of the basement, under the massive white propane tank, was a pond of kerosene and rows of unopened plastic containers of the same.

"That Cal!" Lara cursed. "I should have known."

"From what we have been able to gather from our limited point of view," Dana said, "Cal had merely been coming back after sobering up to apologize for what happened to Mindy. He found you in the snow and carried you back here to the nursing hand of Nell Kutroff. Rach and I tried to shout to him; we could hear them talking upstairs, but Nell had our mouths professionally taped. Cal actually saved your life. For the time being. While you were blissfully defrosting, after Cal left, Nell tied you up and dragged you down here."

"I don't understand," Lara said. "Where have you been?"

"Oh, I've been in the house all along.

After I got back from the lodge, Nell offered me a delicious, steaming cup of cocoa, and I woke up in her closet next to one of my skis, tied and taped like you wouldn't . . . like you are now. Plus my mouth. I heard you calling the lodge, and arguing with Rachael concerning my whereabouts. I appreciated your concern. Man, have I got to pee!" She sniffed. "I see you couldn't wait. You know, Lara, I bought you those pants last Christmas, and you've ruined them."

"How can you joke at a time like this!" Lara cried.

Tears swelled out of Dana's eyes, and Lara could see that she'd been crying already. "What else is there to do?"

Lara turned the other way. "How's your head, Rach?"

"It's felt better. Am I still bleeding?"

"Yes. A lot. What happened?"

"After you left with Percy, Nell and I adjourned our fight to the living room. I thought I was getting the better of it until I turned my back for a sec and felt the poker cracking my skull. I came to down here, and Nell brought Dana down a few minutes later to keep me company."

Lara could not keep up with the revelations. Especially when they left so much unexplained. "I'm so sorry, Rach."

"Don't hassle it. If I had a choice between drinking coffee with Nell or going for a late night stroll with Percy, there wouldn't have been a choice. Did you kiss him? I bet he's a good kisser."

"Just once."

"Who made the first move?"

"He did, of course."

"You liar, Lara, you're hornier than me. But you don't have to apologize; I understand."

"No, I'm sorry because I suspected you as the murderer."

"Me?" Rachael said softly, a sadness in her voice Lara had never heard before. "Not me, Lara. How could you think that of me?"

"I overheard you on the phone."

"Ohh, I see. I was just talking to Ted McDannel. You know, that creep with the mold on his teeth? He did a brake job and a tune-up on my car for free, and to compensate him I invited him over to watch a movie on TV and let him have a small feel, nothing big. Anyway, the movie we watched was *Carrie*. From that he got the idea of a way to fix the balloting for homecoming queen. Ain't I a jerk? I never told you, Lara, I know I'm prettier than you, but in every other way, I've always felt way behind. I didn't think I could win honestly. Since Dana was no longer on the Associated Student Body Council, and Ted was Sergeant at Arms, we figured we could pull it off."

"How exactly were you going to fix the balloting?" Lara asked, knowing it was an absurd question, given the situation.

"You don't want to know."

Lara fought with the tape and string, not getting a quarter of an inch of play. "Rachael, you nut, you would have won hands down. Even I was going to vote for you."

Rachael sighed. "We'll never know now, will we?"

"Where's Nell now?" Lara asked.

"Upstairs," Dana said.

"Celeste! She'll kill Celeste!"

"Lara, she's going to kill all of us," Dana said.

A light bulb exploded in Lara's mind. The glare of the obvious had covered the truth. Celeste had been right.

Don't you know? I think you know. I think you remember.

"Maybe," Lara said.

"What special exempt status does Celeste have?" Rachael asked. "Because she wasn't at the slumber party?"

Lara did not answer, but asked instead: "Rach, I asked you before and I'm going to ask you again. Why did you frown at the Ouija board when it spelled Nicole's name?"

"Lara, I realized that we're all about to be killed, but could you please stick to more pertinent topics."

"That's a weird question," Dana agreed.

"Someone was moving the planchette, wasn't she?"

"We all were," Rachael said.

"But wasn't one person moving it *consciously*?"

Rachael took a moment. "I thought at the time . . . yeah, maybe."

"So what?" Dana asked.

"Probably nothing," Lara said, "possibly everything."

"Someone's coming," Rachael said tightly. "No begging. Don't give her any satisfaction."

There were feet on the steps, moving carefully for they lacked flexibility from being too long in the hospital. Dana and Rachael gasped. Lara didn't. From the moment they had met in the library, a part of her had known.

"Celeste!" Dana cried.

"Untie us!" Rachael said. "Quick!"

Celeste ignored them, having eyes for only Lara. Such beautiful green eyes, like a child's, a child who was never supposed to have grown up.

"Hello, Nicole," Lara said.

Nicole — Celeste — acknowledged her insight with a slight nod. "I tried to tell you."

The truth had been crying for her to notice. The awkwardness when Nell and Celeste "first" met, overcompensating for the fact that they had spent their entire lives together. The prescription cream in the shower, really for Nicole Kutroff. Nell and Celeste's unspoken rapport in charades, not unusual for two who had always been together. Nell's overreaction when Cal had pinched Celeste. A dozen other hints.

"And you didn't want to hurt any of us," Lara said.

Nicole's face changed horribly, innocence fleeing from the memory of years of torment. "I could not hurt you enough," she said bitterly.

Rachael and Dana were shocked speechless. Lara wanted to plead that it had been an accident when Nicole reached down and pulled off her thick sweater. She was naked underneath. Dana began to choke. Rachael closed her eyes. "Oh God," Lara breathed.

Scars of a decade of constant surgery were there; swollen and convoluted red flesh stitched together with only thought for a chance for life — not for what that life may have to be like. Grotesque lumps were her breasts; a tight band of knotted tissue was her abdomen. No nipples, no bellybutton. A touch would bring pain. *I've never gone out with a boy.* The sight brought revulsion.

"I could take off my pants," Nicole said with a feigned laugh. "It gets better, more interesting." Lara shook her head.

"You can't be," Rachael stuttered. "You're dead!"

"Wouldn't that have been better for all of us?" Nicole sneered. "Oh, I wanted to die. And I did, again and again and again, every time the pain shots wore off. My parents told you I was gone because they didn't want anyone to know they had such a *thing* for a daughter. Of course, that's not what they told me. They said that they were trying to give me a chance for a new beginning, a normal life. Hah! Even on the hottest days, even in the backyard, I always had to be totally dressed. They were just ashamed. But it's funny, you know, there were unique compensations. I got to see pictures of my own funeral!"

"You don't want to do this," Lara said with a conviction that came from knowing she spoke the truth. The hate Nicole was trying to project wavered.

"But I do!" Nicole smiled nervously. "I've been waiting for this all my life. I've dreamed about it."

"Not you," Lara said. "I remember —"

"You remember a happy little girl!" Nicole interrupted, turning away, putting a hand on the propane tank, the equivalent of a warhead if there was the tiniest spark.

"Maybe. But what about Celeste? I knew her pretty good."

"Yeah, right, sure," Nicole said sarcastically. "Didn't even know she was a monster, did you?"

"You're not a monster."

"Dana almost threw up! Rachael couldn't even look at me!"

"You were such a good friend. I can't believe —"

144

"It was all an act, Lara! I was never your friend. Never!"

"No one's that good an actor," Lara said. "Do your parents know about this plan? They don't, do they? It was Nell's idea."

"It was my idea!"

"I don't believe you. Why did you come to live with your aunt if you simply wanted to kill us?"

As though she could no longer support herself, Nicole leaned on the tank, her head turned down. "I wanted to know what I was going to destroy."

"No," Lara said, taking an awful gamble, with nothing to lose. "You came because you didn't trust Nell. You wanted to see if we were as rotten as you had been told."

"And you are! All so happy! Going to your football games, and your movies, and out on your dates! Never once thinking about what you had done! I even asked you! Was anyone else hurt? And you said no! You'd forgotten! How could you have forgotten me?"

"It was too painful to talk about," Dana said.

Nicole fought to calm herself, standing away from the tank, staring at all three of them. "I came to live with my aunt to find out why. That's all. Why. I was only a little girl."

"There is no *why*," Rachael said. "It was an accident."

"Lara poured gasoline on me!" Nicole shouted.

"Brandy, she was trying to put you out," Rachael said. "And I did put you out. And I burned my hands doing so."

Nicole shook her head. "That's not how it happened. Nell put me out. Nell saved me."

"Nell tried to," Lara said. "We all tried."

"No! You didn't even want me there. You all hated me!"

Lara decided that the moment had come. "You're wrong, Nicole. Nell was the only one who didn't want you there. She was the one who spelled your name on the Ouija board as the demon. She was the one who pointed the planchette at you. *Nell caused the accident!*"

"Oh really, Lara," Nell said quietly, coming down the steps, dressed for the cold, handing Nicole a down jacket. Lara was struck by how at ease she was, how calm. "You want to go now, Nicole? Mindy's not going to wake up."

"Wait," Nicole said, the opposite of her sister, torn with anxiety. "I want to know exactly what happened."

"I told you," Nell said, moving to the propane tank, checking the pressure gauge, kerosene thick at her feet.

"Liar," Rachael swore.

Nell smiled. "You weren't much fun, Rach. You have no imagination. Lara was the only one who was worth the trouble. She was perfect, obsessed with the missing snowman, Dana's ski, the ash in the ice. That last *omen* was almost too much. It almost frightened her away. You look surprised, Lara. This is the juicy part, you're all pissing in your pants. But I wanted revenge to last, where I could savor it. I wanted to haunt you. With a hand torch, while Rachael and Dana were cleaning out this basement, I melted the snowman. Took two minutes. And it was I who knocked out Dana, and slid down the path on your previous tracks, and planted the ski, and melted the snow, and threw in a bag of ash and bones from an old barbeque."

"How gross," Dana said.

"I was safe," Nell went on without a pause. "I could see you and Mindy still miles away. Everything worked my way. Foolish Cal and his napalm, an accidental plus that helped set the mood. And I even got to light Mindy up! And best of all, my plan worked! I overheard you talking to Percy, Lara. Spontaneous human combustion! Pyro-kinetics! *Carrie!* Your head was in the palm of my hand. You were afraid you'd catch fire any second." Nell pulled a lighter from her pocket. "And you see, you won't be disappointed. This place is going to blow. Nicole and I can hover around the flames, keep warm, until help arrives. And no one will go to jail, for there will be no evidence."

"Wait," Nicole said again, eyeing her sister. "That night, on the Ouija board, did you spell out my name?"

"Of course not."

"Lara said you did."

"At this point, Lara would say pretty much anything," Nell muttered, hardly listening, opening a box containing four more bottles of kerosene. "Give me a hand with this, will you?"

Nicole did not move. "If I hadn't suffered so much —"

"Maybe you would let us go," Lara said.

"She's my sister." Nicole bit her lip, talking to herself. "She took care of me."

"She lied to you," Rachael said.

A flash of anger distorted Nicole's face, but it didn't last. Nell unscrewed a cap and savored the smell as though it were a fine wine. "You poured brandy, not gasoline?" Nicole asked.

"Why would we have gasoline in our living room?" Dana said.

"But brandy's full of alcohol," Nicole moaned.

"I panicked," Lara said. "I used it because it was wet. I just wanted to put you out."

"I suffered so much. . . ." Nicole whispered, squeezing her eyes shut, trembling.

"But you've been happy these last couple of months," Lara pleaded. "Remember when we went to the show, and ate all that chocolate ice cream afterward, and got sick? Remember when the five of us all went —"

"I remember burning!" Nicole wept. "That's all I remember!" She turned on Nell. "Stop that!"

Nell put down her bottle of kerosene and glanced over, unruffled. "Yes, Nicole?"

"I want you to stop."

"We can't go back."

"We are going to stop."

"But —"

"You lied to me! You said that it was gasoline! You said that she poured me with gasoline! On purpose!"

Straining her head as far off the floor as possible in order to follow the exchange, Lara noticed a bulge in her pants beneath her coat. The flare gun! Nell had failed to remove it. Now if she could just get her hands on it, and aim at Nell while she stood in the kerosene.

"You see my face, sister?" Nell said quietly. "It's not very pretty, is it? In fact, it looks like the rest of you. Now look at them. They all look fine. So, who's lying to you?"

"No one has to be lying," Nicole said, obviously fighting a tremendous internal battle. "Before I moved in with Aunt Martha, I told you —"

"That was a mistake, anyway," Nell interrupted. "If these ladies hadn't been such dimwits, they could have traced the Kutroff name through her."

"I'm glad I did! I'm glad I got to see and hear both sides of the story! Nell, we don't have to —"

"Stop!" Nell said, raising her voice for the first time. Nicole cowered. "We will not argue about this again. Go out on the porch. Wait for me. It's already done."

So close, yet with a draining heart Lara saw that it was not to be. Blood was stronger than truth. Nicole bowed to her sister's command, pulling on her sweater, her jacket, limping toward the stairs, not looking at them.

"Good-bye, Celeste," Lara said sadly.

Nicole turned. "Why did you call me that?"

Nell had returned to her kerosene bottles. "Because Celeste was my friend," Lara said. "And because you're not. We were right all along. You've shown us nothing new. Nicole is *dead*."

Nicole's frail shoulders sagged with the burden, and Lara thought she would fall to the floor. Yet suddenly she smiled, as tears watered from her eyes. "Celeste means 'heavenly,' " she murmured, in a far-away space and time. "I picked that name to fool you. Celeste. My mommy has a picture of me in a long, golden dress when I was seven years old. No, I had to have been six. Couldn't wear dresses when I was seven. It's my favorite picture of myself. I have it in my bag if you want to see. . . . But that picture, it's like looking at another person, someone I don't know, someone I'd like to be. That's the real reason I moved to Aunt Martha's, to be that person, to be happy. I was standing by our pool in my dress, laughing happily. My mother took it just before I fell in the pool and ruined the dress. Got all wet, got all burned. Is that why you said, 'Good-bye, Celeste'?" Nicole's expression focused, hardened. "But I didn't actually fall in the pool." She stared at her preoccupied sister. "Nell pushed me in. She ruined my dress. She was always doing things like that. Always."

Nicole came to a decision. Moving swifter and more silently than Lara had ever seen before, she came down the steps. With a finger to her lips, and her eyes glued on Nell, who knelt with her back to them, she removed an unattached hacksaw blade from the pegboard above their heads. In moments she had cut through the tape on Lara's hands. The string was more stubborn. Nicole was working on it when Nell sent her flying with a kick to the ribs. Nicole dropped to the floor like a shot animal, the wind knocked from her lungs.

Nell spat, knocking the hacksaw blade to the corner. "You're no different than them! Get out of here! I should have left you in the fire! You're always getting in the way!"

Nicole was beaten, wheezing, sobbing, nursing her side; she staggered to her feet. Relying upon the railing of the stairs, she tried to pull herself out of the basement.

Disgusted, Nell returned to the corner and grabbed a kerosene container, saying, "For that, ladies, you're going to drink some of this first."

Lara began to rock. Four swings and she had the momentum to sit upright. Her hands were still tied, and it would take time that she didn't have to free them completely; but because of Nicole, they were loose enough to where she could remove the flare gun from her belt. Simultaneously Nell unscrewed the cap of her bottle, and said, "Hot stuff, girls." She moved toward them.

"Damn you to the deepest hell!" Rachael cursed.

"I second that," Dana said, keeping her composure, neither wanting to give Nell the satisfaction.

"Going somewhere, Lara?" Nell asked.

Lara raised the gun, putting four pounds on a five-pound trigger. Nell halted, lifted a penciled eyebrow. She had put on makeup after all. "You're full of tricks, aren't you, Lara? Why don't you shoot?"

"This is a flare gun," Lara said slowly. "Makes a lot of sparks, and you're standing in a puddle of kerosene."

"Fry her!" Rachael said.

"Do it!" Dana urged.

"No!" Nicole cried from the steps, coming back down.

"No one move!" Lara ordered, climbing

to her knees. Nicole paused. Nell smiled.

"Shoot," Nell said. "We can all burn."

"You would go first," Lara said, "and the tank would take time. We could get away."

"Maybe, but you're afraid to chance it," Nell said. "To me, this is nothing new. I am not afraid." She took a step forward.

"Stop!" Nicole screamed. Nell hesitated. "I am afraid!"

"No one has to die," Lara said. "Let me untie the others. We can forget the whole thing."

Nell laughed deeply. "Forget? I'll never forget." She whipped out her lighter.

"It would be worse this time," Lara promised. Another move, and she would pull the trigger. She swore that she would.

"Please, Nell," Nicole begged, actually falling to her knees. "Would you kill me, too?"

Puzzlement flickered across Nell's face. "But this was all for you."

"Don't you see, I don't want it." Nicole wept.

"It would be as though none of this ever happened," Lara said.

For the first time, Nell allowed her madness to surface. "Then I would have nothing to look forward to," she said, eyes dilated, voice dreamy, shuffling slowly toward them. "Nothing to plan, nothing to think about, except how ugly I am." She paused before a dirty round mirror attached to the hot water tank, and smiled at herself, brushing her hair back. Then she wiped at the dust, receiving a clearer reflection, and her face crumpled. "You see this cheek? It's plastic. It's not me."

"Nell, listen to me," Lara said. "We can help you."

Nell picked up the mirror, scrutinizing her features as though for the first time, appalled at what she found. "How would you help me? You're not a doctor."

"By being your friend," Lara said.

"I have no friends." Nell dropped the mirror, a shattered silver array circling her feet. Still she stared at herself in the kerosene-soaked pieces, perhaps trying to arrange them together in a way that made her beautiful. She sighed. "I'll never have a boyfriend."

"Sure you will," Lara said.

"No," Nell shook her head, splintering the glass with her foot. "Never." She struck the flame on her lighter, saying calmly, "And neither will you." And with every trace of lethargy suddenly absent, she pounced. Lara fired at her feet.

The flare shot through Nell's legs, ricocheting off the back wall, landing like a squirming snake in front of Nell on her right, where it detonated. The kerosene lit immediately, swallowing flames engulfing her like a hungry maw. Yet she stood her ground silently, not moving. A glimpse through the incandescence revealed an expression of acceptance. Lara thought she had never seen Nell so peaceful. Up until her childhood friend's face began to melt.

"Nell!!!" Nicole screamed, running clumsily, uselessly to her sister's aid. Lara tried to trip her to stop her, but she was too slow. On the borders of the spreading bonfire, Nicole wavered before plunging her hands, two of the only parts of her body that had not been burned before, foolishly into the flames. Finally dropping to her knees, Nell made a shoving gesture, as if to say get back. Then she fell forward and was lost.

"Nell!!!" Nicole wailed, her heart breaking in the cry.

"Get the hacksaw blade," Rachael said.

"Quickly," Dana added.

Frantically Lara rolled to the corner, banging and bloodying her nose in the process. The binds to her feet took a lot of sweat. Smoke stung her eyes. Finally, she was able to rush to Dana's side. While hacking at the string, Rachael commented. "I knew you wouldn't do me first."

"I won't leave without you," Lara said.

"I might," Dana said. "Hurry!"

Rachael twisted her head toward the propane tank, licked on all sides by the fire. "You owe me one, Nicole," she demanded.

Moving like a zombie, Nicole stood and removed an ordinary saw from the wall above their heads. It was more effective than the loose hacksaw blade. Rachael was freed the same moment Dana was.

"Let's quit this joint!" Rachael shouted, moving Dana in front of her, up the stairs. Lara was on their heels when she realized that Nicole was not following.

"What are you waiting for!?" she yelled, coughing.

"I'm staying," Nicole said, her eyes fixed on the blackened heap that had been her sister.

Lara grabbed Nicole by the ear and yanked her onto the steps. "I'm not in the mood to argue with you!"

Nicole gave no reply. Nevertheless, she cooperated. They had exited the basement and were in the hall heading for the living room and the front door beyond, when a shock wave — had to have been from exploding kerosene bottles, couldn't have been the propane tank — took their feet out from under them. Rachael and Dana backtracked and helped Lara and Nicole up. Lara's leg was on fire. Nicole blotted it out, her hands a terrible sight.

For once, the cold swirling snow was welcome. Rachael stumbled away from the porch and fell down behind a tree, the back of her head still bleeding. Dana ran down the path. Lara helped Nicole to Rachael's side and collapsed herself, pressing a handful of snow on her burned leg.

Rachael bolted upright. "Mindy!"

"I knew we'd forgotten something!" Dana called from somewhere.

"Stay here," Lara said, hugging a tree, pulling herself upright. "I'll get her."

"You'll die," Rachael said, trying to follow, unable to stand.

Lara wobbled toward the porch and the rectangular orange lantern that was the open door. Nicole tried to stop her.

"This was my doing," she said. "I'll get her."

Lara nodded. "We'll get her together."

The fire was spreading from the north wind, which was to their advantage, allowing them to cut through the kitchen and take the back stairs to the top floor. The power was out. Currents of black smoke and dancing red light pursued them. Lara slammed each door shut at her back. It would be a literal hell getting back out — if the propane tank didn't solve that problem for them.

Lara kicked open Mindy's door, shouting into the dark room, "Get up! The house is on fire!"

There came a deep breath, a contented sigh, the resumption of snores. Lara closed the door. Nicole led her to the bed. She felt for Mindy's head, took the glass of water from the nightstand, threw it in her face. "Wake up, Mindy!"

"Not thirsty now," Mindy muttered from a dream.

"Mindy!" Lara touched her eyes. They

were closed. The house trembled as support beams crashed below. "What were those pills!?"

"I don't know!" Nicole shouted over the noise. "They weren't codeine. They were for after operations, real strong. We'll never wake her up. I know."

"We'll carry her." Lara threw off the blankets. "Take her feet. I'll get her head."

"Okay." They stumbled about. Nicole screamed. "Ohhh!!!!"

"What's wrong!?"

"My hands! The skin's coming off!"

"Oh, Nicole. . . . Get back. I'll get her." Lara sat on the bed, and yanked Mindy's listless arms around her neck. But when she tried to stand, her knees turned to mush and she hit the floor in pain that went beyond reason. Who was she fooling? Her leg couldn't even support her own weight.

"Where are you?" Nicole cried.

"Here." Lara rolled over and slapped Mindy across the face. "Wake up, damn you!"

"Sleepytime," Mindy mumbled, hugging her as though she were a pillow.

"Get out of here," Lara ordered Nicole.

"You first."

In a rush of smoke and fiery light, the door burst open. Dana and Rachael stood there, hacking their lungs out. "What are you doing here?" Lara asked.

"One for all, and all for one, and all that

crap," Dana said, grabbing Mindy by the hair.

"I figure that being a hero has got to help me in the homecoming voting," Rachael panted, lifting one of Mindy's feet.

With Dana taking the bulk of the weight, and Nicole leading the way, they carried Mindy in the direction of the living room. Flames whipping up the stairs forced them to reconsider. Even as Lara fought not to panic, she could feel her skin reddening from the heat. Billows of bloody fog engulfed them.

"Any ideas!?" Dana coughed.

"I can't breathe," Nicole gasped, doubling up. Rachael shook her.

"You know this house! Can't we go out a window!? Nicole!"

Nicole nodded weakly. "Lara's room," she croaked.

Fortunately Lara had left her door closed. Once inside, they were able to catch their breath. But in the dark and confusion, the window refused to open.

"Nell locked them all with keys!" Nicole said.

"Out of my way!" Rachael ordered, picking up the desk chair. The crash of glass and the blast of freezing air gave Lara her first real hope that the five of them would see tomorrow. Dana led the way, dragging Mindy by her arms, followed by Rachael and Nicole. The door began to burn. Lara noticed the scarf the snowman had been wearing, lying on her bed. Realizing she was wasting precious seconds, she limped to the bed and, as the floor sagged ten degrees, secured the knitted wool around her neck. Her leap through the jagged window was so hurried that when she hit the icy wooden shingles she immediately fell on her rear end and slid right off the side of the house, burying herself deep in the snow. Moments later Nicole fell out of the sky and landed beside her. Rachael and Dana were dragging Mindy to safety like a side of beef.

"It's going to blow," Nicole said, struggling.

"I feel it, too," Lara said, helping her up.

They were fifty yards from the house, stumbling down a steep incline, when the world erupted in a deafening light. A giant's slap catapulted them head over heels toward suddenly brilliant trees. Lara felt as if she was flying rather than falling, and again briefly wondered if she were dead. Like a flying arrow, she pierced the crest of a drift. When she finally came to a stop and opened her eyes, she saw a spewing volcano top in place of the house. *Right, Nell, no evidence.*

"Hello!" she called.

"Over here!" Dana yelled, off to her right. Lara swam toward them, beginning to think that she must be invincible. The landscape was bathed in an enchanting, shifting blend of yellow, orange, and red, the temperature swiftly climbing. Mindy sat propped up between Dana and Rachael, a mist over half-opened eyes. "Why are you in my room, Lara?" she mumbled.

Rachael asked quietly, "Did Nicole get out?"

"She was right behind me," Lara said, searching. Would this night ever end? If the shock wave had thrown Nicole into a tree. . . .

"I see her!" Rachael exclaimed. "Over there!" She began to reel, putting a hand to her head, sitting down. "You go, Lara. I don't think I want to see."

Lara understood. Near where Nicole lay unmoving, the snow was splattered with blood. The walk to her old friend seemed to take an eternity. Yet as she knelt by the young girl's head, she heard faint moaning. "It's me, Nicole. You're going to be okay."

"I am going to die," she whispered.

Lara squeezed her arms and said, as she had said years before, "I will not let you die."

Nicole smiled. "You told me that before."

Lara nodded. "And I was right, though I never knew it until now."

They were huddled around the unconscious Nicole when the old man with the sunburned face and white moustache walked down from the fires of the ruined house and asked if they would like a ride back to the lodge.

"The colonel," Lara beamed, surfacing from the depths of an exhausted trance. "You've come to rescue us."

He pulled off his gloves and checked Nicole's pulse at the neck, examining her. "This is bad," he muttered, removing his jacket and covering Nicole. "I have a radio in the tractor. I'm calling for a copter. Be back in a moment."

When he returned, Rachael asked him, "How did you get here so quick? The house only blew twenty minutes before you found us."

The colonel began to massage Nicole's legs. "Watching the football game in the bar, I got so drunk by the fourth quarter that I passed out. Can't hold my liquor like I used to. The bartender, Old Ed, he and I go way back. He just let me sleep. So when I woke up it was here in the middle of the night. I was heading back to my place when I stopped by the ranger on duty at the desk to chew the fat for a while. I'm actually retired five years now but I still like to keep my hand in to help pass the days. Anyway, this here fellow — McCormick was his name — was a new guy. I introduced myself, and we got to talking a spell — in fact, he asked if I had moved cars for you gals and I told him that I had — when this tall fellow, a shy over-weight with a swollen jaw, comes in and says that he thought maybe there was some kind of trouble up at your place. He told us how he'd found one of you ladies half dead in the snow and how he'd returned you home but had a funny feeling about it. We gave a call up there but got no answer. Naturally I began to worry and thought I'd better take a ride up in the tractor. That guy — Cal, he called himself — wanted to come also but I wanted to keep room in case I was going to be giving any of you rides back down. Nice fellow, that Cal. Real conscience."

"Sure is," Lara said, thinking that he had probably saved her life twice.

Coming to at the mention of Cal, Mindy said, "I'm his girl friend."

"Oh, God," Dana muttered.

"Which one of you was the one out in the snow?" the colonel asked.

"It was me," Lara said.

"What in heaven's name for?"

"Just for a breather," Lara said, searching the others, shaking her head slightly. "I got lost, wandered too far from the house, then couldn't find my way back."

The colonel nodded in understanding. "That can happen in these storms. But it looks like this one is weakening." A faint glow could be distinguished in the east. He glanced up, a mechanical roar tearing the night, fanning the flames, as a helicopter approached. "A pity, it was a fine old house. Any of you know what happened?"

Rachael went to speak. Lara stopped her with a slashing hand gesture that the colonel didn't see. "We all woke up with the smoke," Lara said. "There was fire everywhere. We don't know where it came from."

"You were all lucky to get out," the colonel said. Suddenly his jaw dropped as his face paled. "My Lord, weren't there six of you?"

"Yes," Lara bowed her head, touching Nicole. "Nell was our other friend. We did everything we could to save her. But it wasn't enough."

Epilogue

Lara leaned against the hospital window on her tender nose, feeling the warmth of the barren sandy landscape beyond. The sky was a hard blue, allowing a clear view of the distant snowcapped peaks. The storm had passed.

"I'm back," Nicole said weakly from the bed.

Lara turned, silencing a pang of sympathy. Suspended on wires from the ceiling, both of Nicole's arms were heavily bandaged. Lara swung on crutches toward the bed. Her own knee needed cartilage surgery. Blood blisters from frostbite tipped her ten fingers. Her burned leg throbbed. Every breath reminded her of her cracked ribs.

"I was hoping that you would wake up before I left," Lara said, sitting on the edge of the bed.

"When is it?"

"Monday afternoon. You're at St. Vincent's, in the valley. You were flown here in an ambulance helicopter. Rachael, Mindy, and I just got discharged today. My mother should be here in minutes to pick us up. How do you feel?"

"I'm alive," she said, shutting her bloodshot eyes. "Did it really happen?"

"Yes."

"Nell's —?"

"She's dead, yes."

Tears, and there would be more in the days to come. "You must hate her, Lara. You must think that she was insane. But to me, to me she was a good sister. She took care of me when I was sick. When I had pain, she would stay up all night and read to me. She wasn't what you think."

"I don't hate her. I was afraid that you would hate me for firing the flare."

Nicole shook her head, grimacing. "I'm going to miss her."

Lara took a tissue and wiped Nicole's cheeks. "So will I."

"Really?"

"I still think of her as a friend," Lara said honestly. Paradoxically, the feeling made the loss easier to bear.

"What did you tell them?" Nicole asked, hesitantly.

"The police know nothing. Officially it was an accident. There was no evidence to say otherwise."

"Thank you. Are my parents here?"

"Yes. They were waiting with me up until a few minutes ago. They went down to the cafeteria for a bite."

"Then they know that you know about me?"

"True. But about Nell, they know the same as the police."

Nicole was worried. "Will it always stay this secret?"

"The four of us have taken a solemn vow, and none of them would dare say a word with the skeletons I could drag out of their closets." Lara hugged her carefully. "In my house, if you like, you can still be Celeste." She kissed her forehead. "I have to go now, but I will come visit in a couple of days."

"Can I call you tonight?"

"Whenever you want." She ran her fingers through Nicole's curly auburn hair, silky like a child's. "How blind I was, only you're this beautiful. I love you, Nicole. I love both of you."

Limping out of the elevator into a hospital lobby, Lara saw Rachael and her mother talking to a handsome young gentleman. Rachael, a white bandage wrapped around the top of her head, had her hand on his shoulder and was laughing.

"Percy!" Lara called.

"Lara!"

She momentarily lost her crutches with his enthusiastic hello. His hug murdered her broken ribs, but it was worth it. "You look a mess," he laughed, gently touching the bandage on her face.

"Thanks a lot!"

"Seriously, are you okay?"

"I had the best brain surgeon on the West Coast. How did you get here?"

"I was so mad at Cal, I didn't talk to him until today. At six this morning, I called your home as we'd planned. Your dad answered. Sounded like I'd woken him up. I almost hung up! That was the first I'd heard of the *accident*." He hung on the last word, waiting, his face an unspoken question.

"It was a terrible accident," Lara said deliberately.

He understood, probably everything. "Always hard to lose a friend." She couldn't think of anything to say. "Anyway, your mother told me she was picking you up today. I sort of invited myself along."

"I'm glad you did."

That helped. "Hi, Mom!" she said.

Lara's mother was a nervous wreck. She shook as they touched, and began to cry when Nell's name was mentioned. So unfair for tragedy to strike their family twice. Lara prayed that Mr. and Mrs. Kutroff didn't appear. Mindy and Dana joined them in the midst of comforting each other. Mindy's arm was in a sling. The doctors promised a minimum of scarring. Dana hadn't even required hospitalization. Though she, too, had ended up ruining one fine pair of pants.

"We'd better hit the road," Dana said, after they had inquired after each other's health. "I have to have the van back by six."

"Mom and you didn't come together?" Lara asked.

"When I heard that she already had company," Dana said, poking Percy, "I thought that I'd better get Rachael myself."

"That was very thoughtful of you," Rachael said, with sugarcoated spikes in her voice.

"You don't have room for me?" Mindy asked.

"Not really," Dana said quickly.

"In a van?" Rachael said.

"We have room for another person," Lara's mother said. "Either of you girls could come back with us."

Lara's eyes rolled at the word *either*.

"Perfect," Dana said. "Mindy, you don't mind riding with them, do you?"

"Noo. . . ."

Rachael frowned. "Why Mindy?"

"Why not Mindy?" Lara asked.

"Why not Percy?" Rachael mimicked. All eyes went to him.

"Hey, leave me out of this," he chuckled.

"Did Cal come with you?" Mindy asked Percy suspiciously.

"Here she goes again," Lara moaned.

"Not with us," Percy said innocently. Dana had developed a sudden fascination with the lighting fixtures on the ceiling.

"Is Cal out in your car?" Mindy demanded of Dana.

"I didn't bring my car," Dana muttered.

"Is he out in your van?"

"Don't be ridiculous, Mindy," Lara said.

Mindy lost her wad of gum, accidently stomped her foot on it. "Is he!?"

Dana was fixing her blouse. "Well. . . ." she began.

The coffee shop all over again.

With the exception of her mother, they all rode home in the back of Dana's van. Never a dull moment.